MINDS WENT WALKING
PAUL KELLY'S SONGS
REIMAGINED

First published 2022 by
FREMANTLE PRESS

Reprinted 2022.

Fremantle Press Inc. trading as Fremantle Press
PO Box 158, North Fremantle, Western Australia, 6159
fremantlepress.com.au

Cover photograph of Paul Kelly by Ben Saunders
Cover design by Nada Backovic, nadabackovic.com
Printed and bound by IPG

 A catalogue record for this
book is available from the
NATIONAL National Library of Australia
LIBRARY

ISBN 9781760991869 (paperback)
ISBN 9781760991876 (ebook)

Department of
Local Government, Sport
and Cultural Industries

GOVERNMENT OF
WESTERN AUSTRALIA

Fremantle Press is supported by the State Government
through the Department of Local Government, Sport
and Cultural Industries.

Fremantle Press respectfully acknowledges the Whadjuk
people of the Noongar nation as the Traditional Owners
and Custodians of the land where we work in Walyalup.

MINDS WENT WALKING
PAUL KELLY'S SONGS REIMAGINED

Curated by
Jock Serong,
Mark Smith and
Neil A. White

 FREMANTLE PRESS

CONTENTS

A WORD FROM THE CURATORS

For many Australians, the songs of Paul Kelly have come to represent tangible links to both time and place: childhood memories, family and friends, first love, first heartbreak, perhaps a reminder of a loved one gone too soon.

These are the spaces where Paul's songs become far more than a melding of words and chords, where a simple line snatched from within a verse or chorus cut like a scythe to lay bare a hidden memory. An instantaneous memory jog that somehow told a story unique to you. Your story. But of course, when heard by another, the same lyrics could tell an entirely different story.

These were the challenges we threw at our talented contributors, who are quite possibly the most spirited and accommodating mob of wordsmiths ever assembled. A huge heartfelt thank you to each and every one of you!

Suitably armed with a Paul Kelly classic, one that spoke directly to each writer, we set them to work. Some coddled their song lovingly, some dissected it with clinical precision, some even grabbed it by the scruff of the neck and sunk a boot in. But in each writer's inimitable style, using the fertile seeds sown over time by Paul, new life blossomed. A reimagining. Fiction, non-fiction, never you mind, for sometimes the line blurs.

As Paul would say, our 'minds went walking'. We certainly hope you enjoy the places, and times, into which they've wandered.

~ Neil, Jock and Mark

WHEN I FIRST MET YOUR MA

YOUR MA

TIM ROGERS

WHEN I FIRST MET YOUR MA

I can't have been the only one who thought it was a lusty paean to the mother of an acquaintance, surely? Even as I write this, I'm not entirely convinced it isn't. Songs, huh? Wily buggers.

This song 'dropped' for me when Paul and I were touring together with Renée Geyer and Vika and Linda Bull. Small houses, hastily written setlists, more cups of tea than I'd ever encountered on tour, and then the requisite, mildly debauched all-nighters. Mid-tour at the Continental in Prahran, nursing a smoky whisky and a smarting heart, I slouched at the bar waiting to join PK onstage when he slid into a version of 'Wide Open Road' by The Triffids that caused me to finally understand its bleak beauty. (Sometimes it takes a new setting to understand a scene.) And then 'Ma'. Simple chords for the intro. G, suspended G … and a verse that was set in a bar – why, quite possibly the one I was slouching in. He tricked the melody a little, beginning in a lower register. A foolish girlfriend, a beautiful friend, a proposal. And then a chorus that felt trite, and a li'l clichéd, but then as my prickly, pickled brain was passing judgement, we're in Fitzroy Gardens and I KNOW that walk, that giddy perambulation. And then another chorus – birds like love, and I understand now about that chorus. It's a pause, a breath to the story. One that allows the 'I know this one!' audience members a chance to warble along, and for listeners to digest the story they're now in. And I was IN. In her father's house, laying with this new love, this wild new story. Walking miles in the Melbourne rain. Rain that never felt as cold or threatening as rain in other cities. But I was new to living in Melbourne then. And even the tap water tasted like a revelation.

Was he talking to his son? His daughters? Well, I've never known. We rarely talk about songs. More likely to talk about a tree, or an old South Australian centre half-forward. But that night after the show at the beautiful Continental, I oafishly blabbed to him about 'Ma' and how I finally 'got it'. He gave that impish grin and handed me a dram, and gave nothing away.

The next time we talked songs was twenty years later in a St Kilda seafood restaurant. I could feel the whole joint craning their necks to hear: 'Bloody hell, PK's talkin' songwriting to some idiot?!' We quickly got back to centre half-forwards.

Melbourne rain still falls softer than any other. You won't convince me otherwise.

THE FASTEST FORD
IN WESTERN AUSTRALIA

JOCK SERONG

TO HER DOOR

THE FASTEST FORD IN WESTERN AUSTRALIA

It was a road song, for my road year. I'd deferred uni and resolved to drive around Australia in my HQ panel van with the unglamorous but reliable 173 cubic inch, redblock motor and a box containing exactly 110 cassette tapes. I had no idea how to change the oil, gap the plugs or even find the jack, but I glued a beer tap on the stick shift and tried to keep the water on my left.

Somewhere in there, among the 110 TDKs, was Paul Kelly's 'To Her Door', released three years previously but still at the forefront of my understanding of relationship breakdown. The rest of the box was almost all raw meat from the suburban pub rock oeuvre: Chisels, Angels, Oils. The Crawl, the Tatts, the Divinyls and the Hunnas. Knowing neither shame nor nuance, I was a devotee of dad-music a full decade and a half in advance of being a dad.

Paul Kelly has never been a notorious mangler of his own lyrics like, say, James Reyne is. Indeed, part of his appeal lies in the utterly convincing, conversational tone of his singing. Undisguised emotion, evidence of lived experience. Not for him the banshee howls of Garrett or the horny tomcat purr of Hutchence on a ballad. So it's been interesting to discover, on re-reading Kelly's words recently (in the excellent *Don't Start Me Talking: Lyrics 1984–2012*), that I'd somehow misunderstood him on several fronts.

It turns out that the bit at the end of the first verse in 'To her Door' where the guitar is louder and you can't hear PK's voice, is the declaration, 'Shove it, Jack, I'm walkin' out your fucking door': a necessary piece of scene setting, since the rest of the song is about getting back in the eponymous door.

I'd missed that, in my screaming on the empty Nullarbor, so I hadn't strictly misunderstood it. But error followed swiftly in its wake. In a rainswept carpark above the kelp of Albany, I shoved the tape in the Kenwood's hungry mouth and I thought, just after she 'thought he sounded better', that *she said I'm underfed*. It turns out that 'she sent him up the fare', which accords much better with her resilient, get-on-with-it attitude than does a throwaway comment about not eating enough, given that by this stage she's been without him for a whole year, and that should have freed up plenty of food money.

But the sending up of the fare, obscured by the imagined complaint about nutrition, led me further into error. I thought his response to her gesture of forgiveness was downright odd: why did he travel *on a limerick* to her door? I've had travelling companions like this and they're insufferable. The Melbourne to Warrnambool train is three hours of social waterboarding: seats that face each other so the guy who does the parts-ordering for the guy who services the shire's auxiliary fleet of executive vehicles can tell you about his junior footy career, down to the formative disappointment of an after-the-siren torp falling agonisingly short in front of the netball team's wing-attack who was wearing a *No Fear* hoodie and a look of timeless, bottomless pity.

So for something like thirty-four years I have wondered at the affection in which Paul Kelly is held as a lyricist when he had been responsible for this lazy instance of shower-whistling, ear-wormery about limericks. Yes, of course I can see now that it was a bus reference, thank you. Travelling 'on Olympic' was a perfectly sensible way to get home.

I pulled into Carnarvon, halfway up the Western Australian coast, low on money and looking for work. Even through my industrial-grade naivety I could see that a job on the prawn trawlers wasn't the answer: along the wharf, scruffy heads appeared in hatchways to tell me I could have a 'tucker trip' (read: we'll feed you and that's all), or I could get fucked.

Thinking the industry was right but the offers were a little short, I took a gig at the town's prawn processing plant, along with a room in the staff quarters out the back. And that's where I met Darryl (not his real name because he might hunt me down) and Ken (also not his real name, and ditto). Darryl and Ken were my next-door neighbours in the staff huts. Darryl was around twenty-five, tall and lean, dark mullet, speed-dealer sunnies. Ken was older, short-cropped silver hair, no teeth and the build of a Staffordshire terrier. He was covered in home-made tattoos, the layout of which reflected his DIY ethic: there were none on his back, and the ones on his thighs were upside down because he'd done them to himself while sitting and drinking. These ones were incomplete (*Fuck the Pol—*), presumably because he'd passed out before he finished. Ken was a trawler skipper, currently between boats. The two of them drank long and hard every night, and their rooms were either side of mine. They alternated venues, and there was no escaping it.

Darryl owned the Fastest Ford in Western Australia. He told me so, many times. I don't know how he could be so certain of this, given we were pre-internet, and in a state the size of Western Australia there were a million places you could hide a slippery Ford. How did he know there wasn't someone with a street-legal GTHO in Meekatharra, or Broome? Darryl's Ford was a '75 XB coupe in a bluey-green colour that had oxidised in the weather, and I couldn't tell you anything about the engine note or even verify how fast it actually was because *it never moved*. The Fastest Ford in Western Australia was as emphatically motionless as the WACA: in fact, it sat on blocks at the end of our row of huts.

Over many long nights drinking beer with Darryl (I can explain: it seemed safer than declining the invitation) he lamented that all he lacked was a new carby, whereupon the coupe would be restored to its mythical status as the FFIWA. He just needed the money. In the meantime, every payday he and Ken would buy themselves a slab-mountain of Emu Export in the handy 750 ml king-brown format and grimly chug their way to oblivion, night after night. The carby would have to wait. *But you should see how fucken quick this thing is, mate.*

So to return to Paul Kelly's argumentative drunk asking himself if he could 'make a picture', well, yes sure – he's trying to visualise his reunited family life. But it was the next bit that led me astray: instead of 'and get them all to fit', I heard *and get the motor fixed*. This made perfect sense to me, as (a) you might recall that in my understanding, he hasn't travelled home on a bus (to wit, 'on Olympic') because he's got a head full of limericks instead, and (b) it follows that what he must be doing is waiting for a carby, like Darryl, so he can drive. The hard towns of remote coastal Australia must be filled with Darryls, composing humorous five-line verse while they worry about the cost of genuine Ford parts.

But then came the fateful day.

I'd avoided the previous night's binge, I don't remember how. But it must have been a classic of the genre, because I was woken in the small hours by a tremendous crashing of glass and a prolonged scream. Now call me a coward, but my immediate response to this was to stay exactly where I was.

Under the blinding lights of the prawn plant early the next morning, among the stainless steel and the dizzying smell of bleach, all was revealed.

Every night, at the end of their binge, Darryl and Ken would carry out a touching act of domesticity. They would stack all their empty king browns just inside the door of the hut, presumably for later transfer to a bin somewhere. On this particular night, Darryl had decided on one last long, sighing horse-piss before bed, to be delivered as always on the lawn outside my window. But on his way out the door he tripped and fell into the assembled ranks of empty bottles and sustained a gigantic laceration to his right arm.

On face value, this was no more than another reason why the FFIWA wasn't going anywhere for a while. But the problem was bigger than that. Darryl's role at the prawn plant was a thing called 'knockout', and it was indispensable to the production process. Only one person did knockout, and that person was Darryl. Knockout entailed standing on the concrete floor in gumboots in front of a steel table with a thick rubber mat on top of it. Every so often a conveyor belt would send down a large steel tray, essentially an ice-cube tray, the contents of which was four deep-frozen blocks of prawns, straight off the trawler. Darryl's job was to swing the tray over his head and slam it on the rubberised table so that the blocks popped out of the tray (anything to get away from Darryl) to be thawed and the prawns sorted. The tray was heavy – I'm guessing about ten kilograms – and Darryl prided himself on his prowess at lifting dozens of them all day long and slamming them with enormous force on the table. It was a job that lacked variation, but he was fond of his biceps.

Such was the bang he made every time the tray hit the table, that every other employee in the place would jump involuntarily. Not knowing precisely when Darryl was going to slam down a block made the torment worse, that, and the endlessly looping *Classic Love Songs* tape on the PA system overhead that carried, like a viral load in its bloodstream, Belinda Carlisle's saccharine horror show 'Summer Rain'.

I got the explanation about the king-brown attack from Beverly, the factory's floor manager. It was seven am. We were meeting in Beverly's office, because under her hairnet she had been doing some thinking.

'You're nineteen, right?' And she was right. 'Wanna make three extra bucks an hour?'

And so I was allocated the hallowed role of knockout. Up till then, I had been assigned a station further down the line from Darryl on knockout: I was responsible for a large steel vat filled with aerated seawater, into which the knocked-out cubes of frozen prawns would slide. I had to stir them around and break them up with my hands so they thawed faster, then sieve them out and send them somewhere else – your barbecue, I guess. The only break from the crushing mundanity was the 'by-catch' that occasionally spun to the surface of the water – spiky juvenile flathead, tiny flounder and crabs.

For this task I was issued white gumboots and a pair of pink dishwashing gloves. The fingertips on these were punctured by dozens of prawn-horns, which would break off in the flesh of my soft suburban fingertips and immediately turn them septic. After a fortnight in the prawn plant, I had lost multiple fingernails.

But by five minutes to eight that morning, my world had opened up. I was standing at the holy of holies, the rubber-matted table, flanked by conveyor belts: one belt to deliver the trays, and one to whisk away my slammed-out cubes of spikes and tails and antennae. And between those belts I saw – or I imagined that I saw – the eyes of my co-workers, sceptically awaiting a new chapter in the deafening history of knockout.

The first tray arrived.

I took it and hefted it overhead. Shit, it was heavy. I smacked it flat on the rubber and it made a deeply unsatisfying thud. Nothing moved. I panicked and swung it again: still nothing. The factory was all a-twitch at the silence. While I stared dumbly at the tray, fingers gradually freezing on its frosty sides, another one came flying down the belt. Backlog. Now I was really in trouble. I thought of home. Through the ammonia I could smell home cooking. I thought of my father making a scotch and dry at our kitchen bench, primary school artwork on the wall behind him. Mum, twisting the ice cubes out of the freezer tray …

Twisting.

I picked up the first tray again and tapped it on one corner. It flexed just enough, and all four cubes fell out. Just like that. I felt like I'd split the atom. I grabbed the second one and the same thing happened. Not even Belinda Carlisle could trouble me now.

By the time Darryl got his stitches out and returned to the floor, I was on record-setting pace. Despite this, there was never any question that my promotion to knockout might be made permanent: everyone understood that this was Darryl's *raison d'être*. He certainly hadn't used the time off to track down a new carby.

He stood beside me at the rubber-matted table and there was a handover of sorts. No, 'Thank you for covering for me during this period of reflection upon my self-defeating behaviours,' but more like, 'Yeah, right, I got it now.'

'But Darryl,' I said, savouring the moment. 'I've discovered the most brilliant thing – you can just tap the corner of the tray and it puts a little twist in it and the cubes just *fall out* – look!' And serendipity delivered a tray to my waiting hands. I gave it a tap and the magic happened.

I don't know what I expected him to do or say. But he grunted and I stood aside and he took up the position. A tray flew down and he grabbed it by the near end with those powerful arms, one bandaged and one not, and he swung it mightily over his head and I saw in that instant his face was contorted in a savage tableau of rage and pleasure as he slammed it flat on the table and the cubes burst from within, and the factory collectively clenched its teeth and Belinda Carlisle went on wailing and wailing about the summer rain.

Like Kelly's star-crossed lovers, Darryl has never aged. They don't have locked-down grandkids. Darryl doesn't have a Prius. He is out there somewhere. Maybe he found that carby and it fed fire to the V8 as he roared away from a stick-up in a swirl of dust and bank notes. But more likely Daryl has ossified, has become a rare constant in a madly shifting world. An entire generation having passed him by, his face still contorts with fury as he slams an endless stream of steel trays on a rubber table. Hundreds of casual packers and sorters have come and gone, lived their lives and raised their children. The Ford still waits on its blocks, cataracts on its headlight-eyes, and dugites coiled in the shade underneath.

The infernal workshop of knockout clocks grimly on, bleach and frost in place of fire. And Daryl is there at its centre, every muscle aching. Walking in slow motion, like he's just been hit.

WITH WALT

MICHELLE WRIGHT

WITH WALT

A woman is driving on a country road. She's been driving for an hour and there's still another three to go. With a stop for lunch and another in the afternoon, she'll arrive in time to have a shower and maybe a quick lie down before dinner. Time to gather her forces.

It's Christmas Day, but the phone call she received last night killed all the merriness she'd been trying so hard to muster. She knew precisely what was coming. The same stale insult her mother-in-law no longer made the slimmest attempt to disguise.

'I'll get you to bring the wine, Patricia. Best if I take care of the food.'

Christmas dinner has always been a loathsome affair, but now she'll be enduring it without her husband. The last time Tricia saw her mother-in-law was at Neil's funeral in March. She managed to avoid a birthday lunch in August by going away for the weekend with her best friend, Maryanne. Christmas is trickier to flee though. And this will be the first family Christmas since Neil's death. Tricia feels obliged, for her daughter's sake, to appear to make an effort.

As she drives, she thinks about Neil for the first time in a week. Or maybe longer. When did that happen? Forgetting she's supposed to miss him? And now as she thinks about him not being there for

Christmas dinner, she wonders if it's really Neil she misses, or just the fact of his existence. Over time, she realises, she'd become adept at using him as a human shield, a bulwark against his mother's barbs. And he'd willingly filled that role at every family gathering for the last thirty-five years.

Neil's two younger brothers, their wives and all their sons will be there at the dinner. And Tricia's daughter, Kate, of course. But Kate is not an ally to be counted on these days. She's the one and only granddaughter, and therefore Granny's little girl. Though no longer a little girl. Thirty-five in January. Expecting her own little girl. And angling for a present of a new car from Granny. And maybe some cash for a babymoon in Bali. Kate worked out long ago which side her bread was buttered on.

Ninety minutes into the trip and the dashboard thermometer reads thirty-six degrees. Through the driver's-side window, the sun bites deep into Tricia's arm. On both sides of the road the rusty, windblown paddocks are frayed as worn-out rugs. With each gust, the sickly shrubs snag desiccated leaves and dust. The road is in need of repair, with crumbled edges and potholes as deep as they are wide. It's only used by locals and truckies trying to avoid the radars. As the car rounds a bend, a livestock transport rolls into view. Tricia turns her head away as it passes. Even before she gave up meat, she couldn't stand the sight of all those pleading eyes.

A few kilometres down the road, she pulls over to eat her lunch in the shade of a long-limbed blue gum. She opens the door and rests her legs on the edge of the wound-down window, then sends her daughter a text, telling her she's on her way. Just as she finishes the message, she hears a high-pitched squeal from behind a tree a few metres further away. She walks towards the sound and stops short at the edge of a shallow ditch.

'Holy shit,' she says. 'Where the hell did you come from?' Lying on its side in the ditch is a pig. Its head is angled towards her, but its eye points up at the sky. Tricia turns and looks along the road to where the livestock truck passed by not long before. 'Did you fall out?' she asks the pig. 'Or did you jump, poor dear?'

The pig is almost as long as Tricia is tall and probably twice as heavy, its skin pale pink, with a thick coat of coarse white hairs. Deep grazes cover the entire length of its flank. Its snout is slightly bent to one side and a deep gash on the top of its head oozes fresh red blood. Tricia takes a step closer and comes into the pig's field of view. Its one visible eye turns and fixes on her. Immediately it starts up a barking grunt, pausing every few seconds to take in a laboured breath. Its snout and bottom jaw tremble with the effort. Tricia takes a step back and slowly lowers herself to the ground. She makes no noise at all, waiting until the pig's grunts become less frantic and its breathing levels out.

'It's okay,' she whispers. The pig's ears twitch. 'I'm not going to hurt you.' She slowly raises her mobile and searches for the number of a veterinary clinic open on Christmas Day. It takes a little while to explain the situation to the woman who answers the phone. There's only one vet on call, she says, and he's busy with emergency surgery. He'll come once he's finished, but that might not be for several hours.

'He doesn't look well at all,' says Tricia. 'He's panting and trembling. His skin is all splotchy.'

'Could you try to keep him comfortable until the vet arrives? The heat won't be helping,' says the woman.

'There's a little bit of shade,' says Tricia, 'but not once the sun moves.'

'If you can cover him with a wet towel or some newspaper, that'll help.'

'Okay,' replies Tricia.

She goes back to the car. On the passenger seat is a patchwork quilt she made for Kate's thirteenth birthday. She brought it in case Kate might want it for the baby. Each square is cut from a piece of clothing she wore as a child – the yellow dress with daisies for her first birthday, the striped overalls with smiley faces on the knees, her prep uniform, her purple velvet skirt. She'd said she loved it when she opened up the wrapping at her birthday party, but Tricia saw she was embarrassed in front of her friends. And when she moved out at twenty-two, she didn't take it with her.

Tricia takes the six bottles of pinot grigio from the boot, opens them one by one and pours them onto the quilt. The wine soaks into the squares of fabric, turning the colours bright, like they were when the clothes were new. She drapes the quilt over her arm and slowly approaches the pig. His eye looks glazed and the skin around it has turned dark pink. From the corner of his mouth, a thick string of saliva stained with blood sags onto the dirt. Tricia kneels by his side and slowly, gently lowers the quilt down onto him. His snout trembles, and then he closes his eye.

It's been an hour and the pig's abdomen looks more swollen, with deep crimson patches under the skin. Tricia calls the vet again.

'There might be internal bleeding,' says the woman. 'The vet will be able to determine that.'

'I think he might be dying,' says Tricia.

'Have you had experience with pigs?' the woman asks.

'No,' replies Tricia. 'But he has the same look as my husband in the hours before he died.'

There is silence on the other end, then the woman clears her throat.

'Well, the vet is still in surgery, but hopefully he won't be long.'

Tricia watches the pig breathing and knows she's right. He's going to die. She's been in this scene before. In the hospital ward where Neil was taken on that final afternoon. After she brought him in through Emergency and they told her that he wouldn't be going home, she had to telephone her daughter to give her the news. How surreal it seemed, and yet so utterly predictable.

And then she'd called her mother-in-law and an hour later, Maureen burst into the room, dragging the young Sri Lankan priest from her parish by the arm. She nodded at Tricia, but didn't say a word to her, then demanded that the priest give Neil last rites. The young man looked uncomfortable.

'Is he Catholic?' he asked Tricia.

She started to reply, but her mother-in-law interrupted. 'He was baptised in the Catholic faith.' She pulled an envelope from her handbag and took out several small black-and-white photos. 'Here,' she said, holding them out to the priest. 'Here's a photo of the christening.' She shuffled through the photos like a deck of cards. 'And here's his First Holy Communion. And his confirmation. His confirmation name is Joseph.'

Tricia had heard Neil speak about his confirmation, but only to say that was when he finally knew he wasn't Catholic.

'Here,' her mother-in-law continued, yanking the hospital tray-table around on its castors and laying the photos out in a row in front of the priest. 'It's clear as day.'

'This isn't a trial, Maureen,' said Tricia, as she slid the photos off the edge of the table and handed them back. She turned to the priest. 'I'm sorry, Father,' she said. 'If my husband could, he would tell you that he doesn't want to receive last rites. He isn't a believer.'

'He was until he met you, Patricia,' said Maureen, a tiny sphere of spit shooting from between her lips.

In the end, Tricia let her mother-in-law get her way. She stood in the doorway while the priest anointed her husband's forehead and muttered the words Maureen was sure would save his non-existent soul. Tricia's eyes were fixed on her husband's face the entire time. She could tell he knew what was going on. She saw the tiny flinching of the muscles around his eyes. When the priest and her mother-in-law left the room, she leaned down until her lips were touching his ear. 'I'm sorry,' she said.

And now, as she kneels in the dirt, from somewhere deep inside her brain come the words of a Whitman poem she studied in a first-year literature class at uni more than forty years ago. She recites the lines aloud.

And I will show that whatever happens to anybody it may be turn'd to beautiful results,
And I will show that nothing can happen more beautiful than death.

Tricia looks down at the pig and lays her hand on the quilt. 'I'll stay with you, Walt,' she says.

As the alcohol evaporates from the quilt, it starts to cool Walt's skin. His breathing is shallow and wheezy, but the look of alarm in his eyes has gone. Tricia thinks of the expression 'piggy-eyed'. How odd that it's used as an insult, she thinks. Walt's eyes are gentle, soft, with long white lashes. Like Santa Claus would have. Tricia talks to him, hoping that the sound of her voice will be soothing, or at least distracting.

'So, Walt, let me tell you how I met my husband,' she begins. 'After I finished high school, I enrolled in an arts degree. I was going to major in literature. I wanted to be a writer, maybe a poet. Neil had just come back to Australia to do his PhD in economics. He'd been working at a bank in South Africa for the last six years. Really, our paths should never have crossed.' She sighs. 'But one day he saw me in the Union Building and he came over and asked me what I was reading. I told him it was *Leaves of Grass* and he seemed interested. Maybe he was at first. When we started dating, I'd sometimes read him a poem and ask him what he thought. He'd try to be enthusiastic, but I knew he didn't really understand my passion for the written word.' Tricia's calves are going numb from kneeling. She sits down on the dirt and straightens her legs before continuing.

'We'd been together about nine months when I fell pregnant. Neil's parents were staunch Catholics, and they insisted we get married, so we did.' She pauses and listens to Walt's breathing. There's a soft gurgling in his throat. She frowns, then goes on with her story. 'When our daughter started primary school, I wanted to go back to university to continue my course, but Neil said it'd be better to study something more practical. He thought kindergarten teaching would be a good option. That way, I could work and still take care of Kate in the afternoons and during the school holidays.'

Tricia lifts her head to the sun and closes her eyes. 'So, in the end, that's what I did.'

A few minutes pass and several huge white cotton-ball clouds float across the sky. Tricia looks up as the first of them moves in front of the sun. The shade on her face is like a cool, wet cloth. Walt must feel it too. He stops panting. His mouth is slightly open and the thick drool is drying on his lips.

'And now Kate's a grown woman,' says Tricia. 'It's hard to believe how quickly the years have disappeared. I'm actually going to be a grandmother soon, Walt.' She smiles. 'It's a strange thing to think of your child having a child. I'm not sure how I'm supposed to feel.' A tear starts to form in the corner of her eye. She shakes her head and it's gone. 'You know how they say it can take a few days to feel that bond with your newborn? Well, Walt, if I'm completely honest, I don't think that ever happened with Kate and me. Not when she was little and even less when she grew up.' Walt blinks and looks straight at Tricia, as if he's waiting for her to go on. 'Kate and her dad were always very tight. Thick as thieves, as they say.' Tricia pauses. She runs her tongue across her bottom lip. It's dry with dust and tastes like blackened toast. 'Sometimes it felt like they were doing it on purpose,' she says. 'To keep me out. But truth be told, I didn't really want to be in on their conversations. I just wasn't interested in the same things they were.' Walt's eye is closed now, but Tricia continues all the same. 'I'm going to tell you something I've never told anyone before, Walt.' She brings her lips close to his ear. She breathes in, the tangy warmth of his skin sharp in her nostrils. 'I think that if Kate wasn't my daughter, I might not want to know her as a person.'

The fluffy clouds are still blocking the sun and the air is not as hot. The quilt has lost some of its dampness but seems to be soothing Walt. Tricia slips her hand slowly underneath. His skin is cooler, but his abdomen is even more distended. He seems to be drifting in and out of sleep. There are long pauses between each breath. Maybe he's drifting in and out of consciousness. She's not sure how to tell the difference. In any case, his breathing is less agitated. She decides to keep talking on the off-chance that it helps.

'You know, Walt, I started to suspect not long ago that the only reason my husband wanted a big, rural property was so that he could spend all his time away from me. He was always outside – mowing, planting, building, repairing.'

Walt slowly opens his eye and a tear rolls from the corner.

'I'm not sure he really loved me actually. Maybe he didn't even like me in the end.' She pauses and pulls the hairs from the sweat on the back of her neck. 'I have a friend called Maryanne who I've caught up with once a month for thirty years. And, when Neil was alive, every time I saw her, she'd ask me the same question – why do you stay with a man who doesn't love you? And I never had an answer for her. But when Neil died, I mean right after he died and I was there looking at him in the bed, that's when it came to me. It was because I thought I needed to love someone, and I didn't have anyone else.' Tricia looks down at Walt. 'That must sound pretty pathetic.'

Walt turns his eye towards Tricia. In it she sees not a trace of judgement. *I don't think it does*, he seems to say.

More clouds have formed. They now fill half the sky. Tricia stands up and walks away from Walt. She calls her daughter to tell her what has happened. It's too late to drive the rest of the way, she tells her. She won't be there for dinner.

'You could still get here in time if you left now,' says Kate.

'No,' says Tricia. 'I don't want to leave him on his own.'

'That is so ridiculous, Mum. It's a pig. What am I supposed to tell Granny?'

'I don't know,' says Tricia. 'Tell her the truth. Or make something up. It makes no difference to me.'

Kate says nothing for several seconds. Tricia hears her breathing, short, sharp outward puffs. She can picture her face. Her lips curled up in a smile of disbelief.

'Alright,' she says. 'But I just want you to know that Granny will be devastated. She really wanted the whole family here today. But that's fine. Whatever.'

Tricia doesn't respond and the line goes dead. She turns off the phone and puts it in her bag. She stands and looks at Walt. As the sun emerges from behind the last of the clouds, it makes the white hairs on his ears glow silver like tinsel. She sits back down beside him, her hand under the edge of the damp quilt, gently caressing his belly.

'It's alright, Walt. I'm more than happy to stay here with you. I didn't want to go to the dinner anyway.' She wipes the sweat from under her chin with the back of her free hand. 'I hate family gatherings. I don't know how to talk to anyone. I don't know what to say to them.' She wipes her hand on her trousers. 'It's just a waste of breath.'

Another hour passes. As a group of cockatoos screech and swoop above them, Walt opens his eye. It has become dull and unfocused. Tricia knows the time for him to die is near. She sits with him for another twenty minutes as his breathing becomes ever slower and more shallow, and then finally, he is gone.

Tricia lifts the quilt, folds it and lays it on the dirt beside her. The sun is below the branches now and is starting to lose its bite. The trunk of the tree glows silver and cream, and the sky is a deeper blue. She leans down and rests her head on Walt's wide flank. He smells of sun-dried grass and sour wine. His skin is damp and warm still, but inside there is silence. On the branches overhead the cockies bounce and click their beaks and tear away at strips of bark. Apart from that, there's nothing. No cars. No trucks. No people. Just the empty road and paddocks. No words or conversations. Not a single human sound.

I'LL BE YOUR LOVER

MIRANDI RIWOE

I'LL BE YOUR LOVER

I'LL BE YOUR LOVER

The program on the television in the Greyhound waiting room is about the Japanese tsunami, and it takes Julie straight back to that afternoon ten years ago. The clink of empties tumbling into the recycling bin. The whir of the fan, industrial in size, metallic paint peeling away to rust. The terrible moist *thunk* as her mother keeled over onto the kitchen floor, felled by her hopelessly clogged heart.

Julie blinks once – can still see her mother's floral dress ruched up at the back revealing spidery veins the colour of port. The cigarette alight, burning a hole into the brown lino. She blinks again until she's back behind the Tropic Coaches counter, Melanie beside her, handing a bloke his ticket to Palm Cove.

Julie considers telling Melanie about her mum, how it's the tenth anniversary of her death but, no, it's something she'd like to keep to herself, as though sparing her mother from an embarrassment. And Melanie won't really care and Julie couldn't stand the blank stare, the murmured platitudes, for such a momentous event. Instead, she points at Melanie's little finger, at a ring with tiny pink stones in the shape of a star.

'Is that new?'

'Yeah,' Melanie says, tossing her fair hair back over her shoulder.

'I bought it for myself when Josh and I broke up.' She admires it, twisting it on her finger to catch the light. 'To remind me to just be myself.' She shrugs. 'To take care of *me*.'

Julie nods, as though she understands. Thinks of the strawberry body butter she treats herself to from the Body Shop, the bag of snack-size Snickers in her pantry. Was that taking care of herself? Is that what Melanie means?

Melanie wears thin rings stacked on each of her fingers, even her left thumb. Most have come from Josh. Julie thinks Melanie got the infinity ring for Christmas, and the band of topazes last Valentine's, but she can't remember if the amethysts were for her birthday or a more random offering of love. Sometimes, like now, Julie points out one of Melanie's rings and asks her about it just to make conversation. It must be a pain for Melanie to dry her fingers after she washes her hands. Julie can't stand the damp that lingers beneath even just her one ring – a small, dark sapphire, oval in shape, that her dad had given her mum on their engagement.

'Well, it's lovely,' she says to Melanie, smiling again at the pink star.

The waiting area is empty, so Julie takes her phone from the shelf, opens Facebook. She looks up her post from two days ago.

Finally got the result for my dodgy hip. Surely I'm too young for this!! Steroid injection next week. Then, Red Arrow, here I come.

She'd tossed up whether to add 'trochanteric bursitis', but that really did make her sound old. Five people have liked the post, and Auntie Beryl has commented:

Oh, Julie, 35 is too young for a hip replacement.

She never reads things right, and her cousin Steve wrote:

Must be from all the marathons you do. With five laughing emojis. He always has to have a dig.

Julie uploads her favourite photo of her mum. It's black-and-white and a little grainy, taken on her wedding day, and she looks beautiful in her red lipstick and pencil-thin eyebrows. The thick veil is pinned to her chestnut hair with a floral arrangement and her dress is lace. Julie still has the dress in the bedroom cupboard at home, and it's tiny. Julie doesn't think it would have ever fit her; not since she was something like eleven or twelve, anyway.

Under the photo she puts one single love heart – the pink trembling one, her favourite – and presses *post*.

She slides the phone into her pocket and, as she glances up at the clock to see if she can go home yet, Tony walks through from the office. He's swapped his driver's uniform for a pair of shorts and a t-shirt.

'Hey, Mel. I just saw Josh outside. I thought you guys had broken up?' His tone is teasing, but he's half frowning too.

'Oh, is he here? I think the idiot wants to try again.'

Tony nods slowly, stares at her a moment as though he's going to ask something, but he turns to Julie instead, says, 'Hey, Julie, do you mind giving me a lift? I came in with Wesley this morning.' He takes his glasses off and wipes the lenses with the hem of his shirt.

She was going to drop into Bunnings on the way home to choose new pavers for the backyard, but she tells him yes. Of course she tells him yes. He's lived in the granny flat beneath her house for nearly four months now, but her pulse still lurches in his presence. She can tell him about her mum on the way home. He'll get it.

'Hey, can you guys drop me home, too?' asks Melanie. 'I wanna avoid Josh.'

Julie nods, forces a smile. 'Of course.' She follows the two of them out through the back door, the warm afternoon light welcome after standing beneath the ghostly fluorescents all day. The day's heat clamps down on her skin, chilled from the air-conditioning.

Tony and Melanie walk ahead, chatting about something to do with craft beer. Tony's about the same height as Melanie, quite short, but Julie thinks he's one of the best-looking fellows she knows. For some reason, in the back of her mind, she equates his lack of stature with what he's told her about his father deserting him and his mum when he was a baby, which always makes her heart cinch.

He says something to Melanie and she throws her head back and screeches with laughter, but Julie thinks she's probably just putting on a show because Josh is glaring at them from across the carpark.

Julie can never quite decide on whether Melanie is pretty or not. She has attractive features, but her nose is perhaps a little too big for her face. Melanie proudly tells everyone that she doesn't bother watching or reading the news, so she can't tell you who runs the country or how many kids Prince William has, but she's smart and confident, knows exactly what words to bandy with the bus drivers, knows that passengers from Mantra Trilogy need to be picked up before the passengers from the Mantra Esplanade, all the things Julie gets so muddled over.

Julie wonders if her mother would have thought Melanie was pretty. Perhaps she'd say Melanie was too brassy for her liking, and she certainly wouldn't approve of how Melanie puts on lipstick in public. But maybe her mum would concede Melanie has a nice smile – that seemed to go a long way with her. And her mum would remind Julie that jealousy is small-minded. Disrespectful to herself and to others.

Julie walks carefully down the steps of the Barron River Hotel, a little wobbly after three and half glasses of house red. It's been raining all evening and they've taken the opportunity of a break in the downpour to leave the pub. The rain has muted the tremendous heat and a few drops splash Julie's forehead as she wanders beneath a fig tree. She stands back to admire the hotel's Queenslander façade, how pretty it looks all lit up against the straggly gloom of Mount Sheridan. Even though her house is close by, her parents had never been the type to haunt the bar, and neither is she, but Melanie dragged them along for a drink on the way home. Julie will never know how Melanie is still standing after all those jugs of beer she shared with Tony, followed by a couple of tequila shots.

Tony opens the door to Melanie's Uber, says, 'Okay, see ya, Mel.'

Mel. There's something so casual, so matey about the shortening of the name that Julie feels a twang of irritation. She bends to wave at Melanie through the window, but Melanie's already turned towards the driver.

Julie joins Tony to walk the short distance to her house and, as they pass her car, he says, 'I'll come back and pick it up for you in the morning.'

She smiles into the darkness, up at the rustling gum trees, and across the train tracks to the hall where she tried out junior gymnastics one sweaty summer. The skin at the nape of her neck, across her throat, tingles in the humidity of the evening. She hugs his words close; it's not often she feels taken care of, not often that someone takes a small inconvenience off her hands. And as she swings along beside Tony, matching the cadence of her step to his, she's reminded of the first time she really noticed him, when her attraction for him had taken hold. They'd both been waiting for

Wesley to lock up the office and she'd caught Tony's silhouette in the corner of her eye, and there was a moment of familiarity – perhaps it had something to do with his height, or the set of his shoulders. She's thought about it since and wonders if she was reminded of standing in her father's shadow. As though she belonged there, by his side.

'My mum died ten years ago today,' she says to him, her voice rising over the engine of a passing truck.

'Julie. That's so sad.' He pauses, peers down at her. 'Was it long after you lost your dad?'

'About four years.' She tells him about her mother's heart, her dad's pancreas.

'Julie, that's so tough.'

They walk up the gravel driveway to her house – to her parents' house. Originally a two-bedroom low-set cottage but now perched high, almost in line with the palm trees. After her mother died, Julie's uncle flew up from Brisbane and helped raise the house and build in the simple granny flat with the life insurance money. For the extra income and the security of company, he'd explained. But the first couple who'd rented the space from her were drug takers and she sometimes missed small amounts of money and trinkets from the back deck. The second tenant was a woman who came with a boisterous staffy that constantly headbutted the fence until palings popped out. There were periods in between tenants when she couldn't be bothered with the hassle and she'd used the space for different hobbies – a spate of acrylic painting, the arrangement of topiary trees, a mini home gym. She'd just sold off the dusty exercise bike and weights when she heard at work that one of the new drivers, Tony, was searching for accommodation.

The floodlights pop on. 'I'll go drown my sorrows in some cooking brandy,' she jokes, her foot on the bottom step.

'Want a beer? It's shit beer my brother left in the fridge, but you're welcome to come in and have some.'

Julie shakes her head, laughs and thanks him, but no. 'I've got work in the morning. Better get some sleep.' But her thoughts are a staccato beat behind the words: she couldn't possibly put him out, and she's so much older than him, and she likes him a lot, but would she ever really take this thing any further, and he's probably just being friendly. She can't tell.

'Yeah, you're probably right. I start at seven.' He waves once and walks around the side of the house to the granny flat door.

The frayed banana leaves are black against the slate sky, and a bat flutters amongst the branches of the mango tree. Reg, the bluey next door, barks at them through the fence.

Still feeling buoyant from the wine, Julie congratulates herself as she unlocks the front door. She feels good, relieved even, that she turned down Tony's offer of a drink, showing him and herself that she isn't desperate. Surely he was just being friendly, too, not actually asking her 'in for a drink'. And she has a hazy idea that she's saved herself from some future mortification – something to do with her age, or depilatory status or, worse, her dodgy hip might have failed her in some unknown way.

She flicks on the lounge room light, and a gecko scuttles back behind the painting of plum blossoms her grandparents had brought back from a Hong Kong cruise long ago. Mould, like a heat rash, prickles darkly across the wall behind the television.

She perches on the side of the couch and checks Facebook.

She has seven notifications. A post on the Stratford page about the hairdresser's opening hours, and four hearts and one like for the post about her mum. There's a comment from her uncle.

Still miss her heaps, love. We'll be up your way for a spot of fishing in the new year.

She thinks of that first dreadful year. Hurting so hard, she'd wondered why there weren't more bereft people just walking down the streets weeping. She'd always considered her mum her best friend, but now, sometimes, only very rarely, she is so lonely she catches herself feeling a little resentful that she hasn't managed to make close friendships beyond her mother. But she is being unfair. She can't be sure what came first. Was she so awkward she couldn't make friends so her mum stepped in, or had she seemed weird to the other kids because her own mother had taught her to be her friend?

Julie settles back into the cushions, turns on the television. She scene-skips to the end of the DVD, pausing just in time for the train scene, when John Thornton catches sight of Margaret. His eyes, his joy. 'You're coming home with me?' he says, and Julie watches the rest of the scene until the lovers are snug together in the carriage and the ache she feels inside surges with the music score. She presses rewind and watches the whole scene again. Wonders if someone like Tony could ever look at her like that. Like a lover. She clamps her hand over her mouth and considers this word she has never said.

She gets up and walks over to the internal stairs, gazing down to where the laundry joins her part of the house to his. Perhaps, when she declined Tony's offer of a beer, she missed her one chance to become closer to him. She's blown it. Regret flares in her chest, and she thinks that the only way to douse it is to have another drink. She yanks open the refrigerator door and brings out the seven-dollar rosé she'd bought for a chicken recipe she'd saved from a Coles catalogue, and pours herself a glass.

But the heat of the wine doesn't calm her thoughts. Instead, she feels the grief sink in, swirling, grabbing on to other disappointments it catches in its desperate plunge through her body – for being left alone, for not at least keeping the exercise bike, for not travelling to Scotland with her cousin, for being too old for Tony. But he's in his late twenties – twenty-seven? Twenty-eight? Is there really such a difference between late twenties and early thirties? She should've taken the beer. She should've. She has another gulp of wine. Her mum used to say that regret's a total waste of time. It's in the past. It's done. And Julie sees the sense in her mother's words, but sometimes, sometimes, she wonders if it's enough to just let go.

The rain picks up again, clanging on the tin roof, splattering the jades neatly potted on the deck. So loud she can barely think straight as she kicks off her shoes and creeps down the timber stairs, sticking to the sides where she knows they won't creak. Her heart thrums from too much alcohol and adrenaline. Just beyond the washing machine, the door to Tony's flat is ajar, a soft shaft of light beaming through the gap. She swallows more wine and moves forward. If he catches her, she'll show him her glass, say she was up for a nightcap after all. The tidal pull of him is so strong, she knows he will understand. He must feel it.

She pads past his bathroom – he's left the light on – and peeps into his bedroom, her eyes slowly adjusting to the shadows. He's lying on his back, snoring softly, arm flung out over the side of the bed.

Julie stares at him, both willing him to feel her presence and ready to flee in fright. She watches him breathe in and out five times and then, slowly, she turns back.

As she passes his bathroom, she notices a blister pack of capsules on the bench. Each capsule half dark green, half pear green. Lovan. She glances back at Tony, wondering what the medication is for. She passes through the laundry, careful to leave the door a little ajar, and makes her way back upstairs.

She fills her glass again and, leaning on the kitchen bench, she looks up Lovan on her phone. Her eyes scan words like *depression*, *fluoxetine*, *antidepressant*, and as far as her wine-addled brain can make out, Lovan is much the same as the Prozac she takes. She smiles. This is something they can build upon. The Prozac's a bit embarrassing, but if someone as cheerful, as nice, as Tony is also on an antidepressant, then it must be fine. Although, perhaps, like Julie, he hides his medication from others, worries too, that others might think he's unbalanced, weak. Or highly strung, like Dr Peterson said.

Tony's secret is like hers. Tony's secret is hers.

She's pleased. Much too wired-up to sleep. But there's a heaviness in her chest too, and she can't tell if it's heartache, heart disease or anxiety.

The afternoon sun glints across the screen of her phone, but she can see the text is from Tony, so she strips off the kitchen gloves to read it. He's at the gym or something; she'd watched his Hilux back out of the driveway a couple of hours before.

Hey Juls we should grab a pizza at Gianni's before Wes's party.

Juls. She takes a deep breath in, thrilled. *Juls.* She wanders out to the deck, the phone still clutched between her fingers. Lorikeets squabble in the paperbark down the back of the yard.

She presses her lips together and sinks into a cane chair, staring at the text. Her instinct is to type, *yes, of course, thanks,* but she holds off. She doesn't want to seem too eager. Like she's waiting by her phone for him to text. She shoves the phone into her back pocket and returns to the lounge room where she pulls on the gloves again, squeezes out the sponge. Spraying bleach onto the wall, she scrubs at the mould, edging her way behind the television unit. The bleach makes her face itch a little, and she rubs her cheek against her shoulder. Stripping off the gloves again, she looks at her phone. Six minutes. That's enough. She types *sure sounds good.*

In the back of the Uber, Julie feels all sparkly inside. Her knees gravitate towards Tony and she has to keep pulling them forward. As they drive down Grafton Street, she points across him, says, 'Look! In the shop window! It's my skirt.' She laughs and sits back again, but her hand rests between them on the seat and his hand is there too and, fleetingly, their little fingers touch, but she doesn't snatch her hand away. She just keeps looking out her window. She doesn't want to appear jumpy or awkward, but also, it feels nice. It's something she tucks away in her mind to revisit and delight in later.

It's drizzling and they dash from the Uber into Gianni's, and it feels so much like a date Julie swallows down a giggle. The waiter directs them to a table for two against the wall. A mirror runs along the length of the room and she glances at herself, checks her skirt is straight, pulls in her tummy. Her hair is cropped, a bit longer than her mother's had been – her mum said it was called a Lady Diana haircut back in its day.

Tony takes off his glasses to wipe away some raindrops and she decides that, actually, he is better looking with them on and, not for the first time, she wonders what it would be like to kiss him; she wonders about the mechanics of it. Would his glasses get in the way, or would he take them off?

They order a mushroom pizza and a pepperoni, and while they wait for them to arrive, he asks her how she is. 'I saw your post about your mum.'

She says she's fine, it's always a difficult time. She tells him with a small laugh about how she's always surprised that more people aren't just walking around weeping. The waiter brings them their wine, and Tony takes a couple of sips and says, 'You know, I had a really hard time after I broke up with my fiancée a year ago. The doc gave me some meds. They've really helped.'

Julie looks at him while the waiter places the mushroom pizza between them, thinking of the green capsules. She considers telling him she is also on meds but instead, between bites, she talks about all the work her parents did around the house. How her dad planted the pawpaws and built the fence, and how the oven in the kitchen is the very same one they chose in the eighties and how much her mum had loved birds, enticing them onto the back deck with bread and honey and little balls of mince.

'Did she put in that bird bath?' he asks, folding half a piece of pizza into his mouth.

'Yes! She did the mosaic on it too. She loved to mosaic. I have a table on the deck that she made as well.'

He reaches across so that his hand is flat on the table between her plate and glass and, without thinking, she almost places her hand over his. She has to clasp her hands together in her lap.

'I know what you should do,' he says. 'You should take up

mosaicking like your mum did. You can make something for the backyard.'

'Oh, yeah,' she says, pleased with the idea. 'I was thinking of doing a little barbecue area out there.'

His phone pings on the table and he turns it over to look.

'Oh, it's Mel.' His face softens into a smile. 'She wants me to meet her for a drink before the party. You don't mind if I go, do you, Juls?'

'Of course not!' Pizza dough lodges in her oesophagus, but she beams at him, taps her own phone. 'I'll just check my messages and finish my wine.'

He half stands and digs around for his wallet before placing a fifty on the table. 'I'll shout the pizza.'

'Oh, no, don't do that!'

But he insists, and she's smiling, laughing even when he says that he and Mel might be late to the party, and she gives him a knowing look, until he's gone and she's sitting alone at the table.

The waiter clears Tony's plate, asks Julie if she'd like to box the rest of the pizza. He goes to take Tony's half-finished wine, but she puts her hand out, asks him to leave it. He shrugs, returns to the kitchen and Julie picks up her phone. Opening Facebook, she scrolls through several posts, but it's hard to read them through the blur. She uploads a photo of her backyard, adds *Can't wait to buy pavers tomorrow to finally set up a barbecue patio area.*

She posts the image and slips the phone into her purse. Leaning back in her chair, she stares at the wine Tony has left behind. She slides his glass towards herself, searching out smudges near the rim. She lifts the glass to her mouth and presses her lips to where his have been.

FIVE-EIGHT

ZOË BRADLEY

FIVE-EIGHT

It's a mistake. Anna knows that much from the start. Tom's home town is faded, smaller somehow than it had been years ago. It's the first thing she notices as she pulls in off the highway, her palms turning sweaty in the afternoon sun.

The Blarney sits proud at the end of the town's main street, the decades-old paint job flaking off like white caps across the pub's façade. Anna pulls into the curb, checks her phone again for the start time. She fossicks in her handbag for a Xanax and swallows one dry so she can feel the pill inch its way to her gut. She rolls down the window, hears the faint sound of conversation and cutlery in the courtyard. She thinks again about blowing the whole thing off, turning round and going home.

It's dark inside and it takes her a moment to notice the few men perched at the front bar who turn for a moment from the footy blaring on the TV. Anna bows her head, slips by them and into the bathroom. It's empty, thankfully, the sound of her boots echoing on the tiles. The wood panelling over the basin is scratched back with names and initials, the odd love heart and phone number. She traces her finger across the top of the hairdryer, to her own name there above Tom's. She thumbs the groove she made with the back of an earring once. She'd only known Tom a month then but it felt good to mark herself into the world like that, to lay claim to the very idea of existence, of being desired. If she squints hard enough she can see a reflection of herself at seventeen. Eyes rimmed with black kohl, so thick they stood out beady like a bird's – wild and alert. Her stomach pulls tight. She'd once read that the body reacts to fear and excitement in the same way, has long missed that flighty feeling, dulled now. She pulls a strand of hair back behind her ear, gives the mirror one last smile, makes it gentler, softer, guiltier.

The band room is darker than the front bar, its windows blacked out with thick blue curtains. The conversation is nearly as loud as the music, different now to years ago when the band got bigger gigs than afternoon background noise slots.

Anna wipes her palms against her jeans, picks a path through the crowd. She lets her hips drop with each step, trying to find confidence in someone else's gait, and it helps for a moment until the top of Tom's head is revealed. He's there behind the amps and mic stands, holding the beat steady as Jimmy wails into the crowd. Even before she can really see his face, it sucks the air out of her. She pushes her way forward some more, until she can see all of him – his foot thumping down on the base, the way his head rears up at the end of each verse, straw-blond hair falling from his face as he does. Everyone else looks the same, though older now. Jimmy has a gut, which pleases her. His skinny jeans strain at the zip below his sweat-stained t-shirt as he takes the mic up in his grasp like a lover's face.

By the stage there's a group of kids no older than she was when she'd first met Tom. They lean into each other, their eyes foggy, hands borderless. The air around them is charged the way it always was in that liminal space, and Anna feels a pang of jealousy.

As she collects a glass of wine from the bar, Jimmy introduces the last song. It's a cover. The crowd belts out the words so there's no tune, just shouted sounds, the same words on Anna's lips, pressed up against the edge of her wine glass. When the song ends, the guys throw their hands up in thanks, yank their leads out and head to the bar themselves. It doesn't take long for the crowd to file out into the courtyard, for it to fill with smoke, but Tom's still there, steady fingers unscrewing the kit, always the last to leave the stage. The leather jacket they bought together at the Vic Markets creases like skin as he twists back and forth pulling everything apart.

Anna sucks down the last of her wine, clutching her bag to her clavicle, until the final few people drain out. Sometimes she wonders whether too much has changed for her to be recognised, maybe hopes it has. But as he leans over to dismantle the cymbal, he squints through the stage lights in her direction. Anna places her wine glass on the bar, holds her hand up in a wave as he approaches.

'Hoped that was you,' he says, reaching up to brush the hair from his face. He pauses, smiling, looking for permission as he pulls her into his chest. His t-shirt is wet through, but she lets him hold her there, pressed up against the familiar shape of him.

Someone calls out from the other side of the bar towards them. It's Jimmy. He motions for Tom to join the rest of the band, who've been encircled by a group of women her own age, their hair straightened and bleached so deeply it doesn't move.

Tom pulls back and looks Anna over, his initial smile faltering.

Anna feels small and sober, thinks again about driving back to the city.

'You wanna go to the bluff?'

Tom's still got the same Holden station wagon – dark blue enamel that always reminded Anna of the deepest part of the ocean where you can't see the sand. She fills her lungs with stale air – self-rolled cigarettes and the animal skin of his drums – as grey clouds roll in over the windscreen. They've forecast a storm, great flashing signs all along the freeway on her way down. Tom guides the car through the early evening streets, the traffic lights bright against the blackening sky, and pulls into the bluff's car park. He brings the car to a stop, the gravel growling under the tyres. Neither of them has said much – he punctures the silence to apologise about the old takeaway wrappers in the footwell; to ask if she's cold. He's slow as he pulls up the handbrake.

'Haven't been back here for ages.' He waits a moment before putting his hand on hers in the passenger seat. She lets his fingers sink between her own. When she turns to him, his mouth is twitching at the corner.

It's been nine years, and it surprises her still how often she sees him in the streets, finds his features in strangers so clear that for a moment she can feel the full force of their reunion. At first it was easier to replace his face with every person who held their hands against her skin. But now it was habit.

Out of town, the wind is stronger. The waves flex up in great walls, lashing the breakwater and showering the cars with a fine sea mist.

Anna closes the car door and puts her arms around herself. Tom ducks into the back seat and hands her an old jumper. The smell of him in the wool makes her stomach lurch.

There are people coming back from the track down to the blowholes. They're wearing polar fleece, matching sneakers. The man tells Tom it's wild out today, tells them both to be careful.

'Rocks slippery as ice,' he says.

Anna and Tom nod in unison, and Anna feels that remnant part of them pulse, like a once-flexed muscle flickering to life. There had been a time when she'd imagined them like this, bands on their fingers, growing old side by side.

'You've grown bloody tentacles into me,' he'd said one night, the two of them sharing a joint on his couch. 'Like this fish I learned about in bio at school. Crawled right up some guy's wang and wouldn't come out. The guy cried when he pissed.'

Anna had laughed, puckered her lips and climbed onto his lap, making smacking noises, like a fish, in his face.

They spent most weekends this way – holed up at his shack or out on the road, sleeping in beach parking lots, cutting back and forth to follow the coast. Tom would turn the radio up so loud the car doors shook, tapping out the beat on the steering wheel and on Anna's thigh.

She asked him to teach her once, sat with him at the kit as he held her wrists and showed her a simple five-eight. Each time she found him practising, she would make her way to his lap like this, let him throw her arms around the Sonor, watching her hands make a sound they couldn't on their own.

Tom places his hand lightly against the small of Anna's back, bracing her as he guides them down the boardwalk and into the headwind. The ocean below the rock face heaves, its surface choppy. They say this bay is full of shipwrecks, that it's constantly churning for the lives cut short, or the rotting masts that disturb the water's natural flow. She remembers weekends down here lying in the back of Tom's car, wrapped up in each other all night, the anger of the ocean in their ears.

Ahead of her Tom navigates the rocks out to the blowholes, his limbs echoing those sure movements from years ago. He must be forty now, like her, and when he turns back, Anna catches the fine lines etched into the corners of his eyes, like the fibres in his drum skins, translucent – all the workings of him revealed. Anna holds the cliff to steady herself, runs her hands along the scars in the rock, hollowed by seawater and storms.

They'd met in town, at the peak of his career. She hadn't known the band, just liked the way it threw her and her friends around that old band room. There was something in Tom from the start for Anna. Something about the way his footfall reverberated in the room, in her. She'd found him outside later having a smoke between sets, still remembers the way he lit her one, so close she could smell the beer on his breath.

They find a mostly dry spot and perch there to watch the water throw itself into the rocks and then recede over and over. Every now and then it sprays them with fat, icy droplets. In summers past, they would lie right there, the warmth of the rock on their backs, and wait for the blowholes to burst, for the water to arc over them.

He's with Sara now, she knows that much from the photos she's found on his profile. No kids yet, no wedding – it's a thought she likes to hover on sometimes. Every now and then she logs on to see what they're up to, whose party they're at, Sara playing out life in her place. It's how she knew he'd be alone this weekend.

They manage to navigate conversation without needing to mention the obvious, talking instead about work – drum school for him, some shitty office job for her. She doesn't mention the two kids that split her open, though she imagines he's heard somehow, or can sense it at least.

They sit like that, knees gravitating towards each other, as the waves thrash and fold back into foam. When the winter sun starts to bleed into the horizon, Anna pulls him back to the car.

Tom's shack hasn't changed since the weekends she spent in his old t-shirts. It smells of boy – old pizza boxes stacked up against the recycling bin.

She eyes the spices on his shelf. The labels she'd made one weekend when she thought that kind of domestic order could prolong them.

Anna smiles. 'I've missed this place.'

'Coulda come back any time you liked.'

She nods an inch like everything in her head's going to spill over.

Tom gets the wine glasses from the cupboard, sucking in his gut as he reaches up. He hands her a glass, leads her through to the backroom.

The old Sonor is still set up by the dining table, which is pushed back against the wall.

Anna places her wine down and takes a seat on the stool. She picks up the sticks from the floor and holds them out to Tom. He straddles the stool and she puts her hands in his. They play a simple five-eight that she feels in her chest, like being in the middle of a thunderstorm. Tom rests his chin in the crook of her neck, and she drops the sticks.

His bedroom is dark, a dampness creeping in from the skirting boards. When he collapses, short breaths at her ear, she senses a hollowness, even as his arms close around her.

He pulls her in closer, kisses her temple. Anna wraps the doona around them, listens to the faint sound of a wave being sucked back out to sea. She waits, at first for the right words, then for him to say something instead. But his mouth slackens, his breath humming sleepily against his lips.

Anna doesn't sleep. The night is long, cut up into every one of his snores, his sleepy hand finding her across the bed.

When dull light starts to seep through the blinds, the weekend is already over. Anna slips out of bed, finds the old percolator and fingers the marks they made when they left it on the stove without anything in it once.

They'd been having an argument. In those last few years they'd fought constantly – the girls that hung around after shows, the fact he hardly made enough to cover rent, the amount of weed he put away. They still found each other every night in the dark, even that morning when she finally told him she'd found a place back in the city.

By the time Tom wakes, the day is getting older and reeks of hopelessness, the way Sundays do. They drink bitter coffee on the front porch as the sky fills with clouds.

Tom grinds his cigarette into the concrete at his feet. Anna takes a long drag of her own, sucks it right down into her belly.

'Guess you'll be getting back then?' he says, collecting up their stained mugs.

In the midday light, she catches a flash of Tom she doesn't recognise, wonders whether the greatest heartache is finding these details in a memory you thought you could contain.

On the way home, the clouds grow darker. At the first set of lights as she hits the outskirts of the city, Anna takes her wedding ring from the glove box and slides it back onto her finger. The storm they promised never comes.

IT STARTED
WITH A KISS

NEIL A. WHITE

IT STARTED WITH A KISS

IT STARTED WITH A KISS

A rush of cold air hurried me through the front door and ruffled the pages of the hostess's reservations list. Young, attractive and with a cuticle causing her some angst, she belatedly conjured up a smile and asked my name.

'Baxter. Reservation for two.'

I'd arrived early, as was my wont, and surveyed the room. I searched for faces that quickly turned away. Checked for choke points. An exit strategy if it all went to hell. Situational awareness the instructors called it. Military training still ingrained in my every move. I smiled grimly and attempted to shake off my building anxiety. I was a long way from Anbar Province. Both in miles and years. There was no IED in the bread basket. No weapon beneath the napkin draped over the waiter's arm. My war may have ended a lifetime ago, but habits were hard to break.

A quick glance at the image on my phone confirmed my analysis: she'd yet to arrive.

'Would you like to be seated?'

I didn't think the hostess was asking the cuticle she'd resumed picking, so I answered.

'I'll wait at the bar.'

Votive candles flickered atop empty tables as I sidled past. Slumping onto a richly upholstered stool, I stared at a row of whisky bottles. A mirrored backdrop provided a view of the tables at my back. More situational awareness. When the bartender appeared, I ordered a double.

A tranquil gloominess tinged with a creeping sense of disquiet enveloped the room. Like a watering hole at dusk. Waiters scurried past like foraging army ants. In a loose circle, hyenas dressed in Armani suits laughed at nothing in particular. And from the deepest shadows, cougars with lips pumped full of botox eyed their prey.

Beads of sweat raced down my spine. My left foot bounced nervously on the bar's foot rail. Pins and needles scurried from fingers to forearms. I'd felt less anxiety on patrol. Back then, at least, someone had my back.

I drained the Scotch for a dose of courage and checked my phone. Perhaps she'd cancelled, stricken by a case of cold feet worse than mine. It'd taken years to get to this point. Countless therapy sessions to confront my fears. Most real. Some imagined. Simply to trust all I touched didn't die.

No new messages. I switched over to the dating app and the radiant smile of a dark-haired goddess appeared. Too many years my junior. Light-years out of my depth. And the pure folly of tonight's meeting came crashing down.

'Waiting on someone?'

A slim redhead had slipped onto the barstool two down from mine. Smartly dressed. Attractive. Alone. An expectant smile waiting for a reply.

'Ah, yeah.'

'Hot date?'

Her lilting voice helped soothe my nerves. A momentary respite from an impending calamity. Forestalling my instinct to cut and run.

'The way I'm sweating, I guess so.'

She toyed with a gold chain hanging around her neck and laughed lyrically. Burgundy nail polish matched the shade of her blouse. A plunging neckline revealed a modest cleavage and smooth skin the colour of alabaster.

'Louise.'

'No, her name is—'

'I meant … my name is Louise.'

'Oh, sorry. William.'

Louise leaned closer and extended a hand. I caught a faint scent of spring flowers. Noticed long, delicate fingers. I held them gently. Afraid my rough skin and gnarled bones may do everlasting damage. Knowing it wouldn't be the first time.

'Pleased to meet you, William.'

Her head tilted to the left. An inquisitive expression played on her lips and furrowed her brow.

'William, hmm. Sounds quite formal. Not Will, perhaps Bill? Never Billy, by chance?'

I watched my finger complete a slow circuit around the rim of my glass.

'Friends called me Billy back in school. But a lot of water …'

A deep sigh completed the sentence for me.

'I'd like to think I've grown since those days. Matured.'

A slight change of name. A change of scenery. Creating a new persona. If only the past was that easy to erase.

Louise gazed into the near distance and let the silence linger.

Apparently, I wasn't the only one with an abundance of baggage to lug around. But as if a switch had been flipped, a smile suddenly lit up her face.

'So … William, definitely not Billy. You the victim of one of these Tinder traps, too?'

'How'd you know?'

A slight pause. Her features frozen in time. Then a smile as her head tilted once more to the left.

'I see it there on your phone. Swipe right for your heart's delight.'

I slipped the phone hurriedly into my pocket. Felt the rush of blood to my face. Unsure why.

'Funny. You work in advertising?'

It wasn't my first guess at her profession. It was the glitzy bars in the city centre where the high-priced hookers usually plied their trade, not mid-range steak joints in the 'burbs. An old buddy swore by them. Hookers, that is. Though he did enjoy a good steak. Preferring to lease rather than buy, as he called it. Cheaper in the long run, he claimed. I'd leased on occasion. Had no problem with buying. Though my life history had done a number on my credit score.

'Advertising? Definitely not. And though I hate these contrived meetings, how else are people our age to meet these days?'

Our age? Not from where I sat. Long, lustrous red hair. Dainty upturned nose. High cheekbones. Full lips painted stop-sign red. The only blemish, beginnings of crow's feet branching away from emerald-green eyes. Otherwise, perfection. Perhaps she'd had some work done, a coloured rinse to wash away the grey, but in the dim ambient light it was impossible to tell. And knowing what faced me in the bathroom mirror, who was I to complain?

'Not sure about your judgement regarding age.'

'You're too kind. Can I buy you a drink?'

'Sure.'

Louise ordered another Scotch, a glass of the house white for herself, and motioned to the stool next to mine.

'Mind?'

'Feel free.'

I smiled but my instincts remained on high alert. Once again, I wondered if she was on the game, but found myself willing to play along. Nothing ventured …

'To new acquaintances.'

'Cheers.'

As our glasses met, Louise looked deep into my eyes. And something passed between us. A stirring in my soul. Warmth. Understanding.

Or perhaps just my libido joining the conversation.

'Have you travelled, William?'

The spell broken. Composure regained.

'Far too much.'

'Really, how so?'

'Where to begin …'

But, begin I did. An hour flew by in the blink of an eye. When the waiter interrupted to ask if we wished to be seated, I realised the dark-haired goddess must have made other plans.

'Looks like we've both been stood up, William.'

'Care to join me for dinner?'

The words tumbled from my mouth before I could swallow them. And with it my chance to scurry back into hiding.

'I'd love to.'

I smiled. Aimed for charming. Hoped to avoid lascivious.

The waiter led us to a table tucked away in the corner. I followed the sway of her hips. Politely held the back of her chair while she sat. Laid a hand gently on her shoulder.

While Louise toyed with her napkin and straightened her silverware, I buried my nose in the menu. A cursory glance was all I needed. New York strip. Recon mission complete. Forever a creature of habit. However, Louise – head tilted to one side – perused the selections with an almost childlike wonderment.

'So many choices. What would you recommend?'

'You prefer meat or fish?'

'Fish. And would you order? I'm not good at ...'

Her voice faded to a whisper as if her words held a deeper meaning. Then her smile returned and I busied myself in making a selection.

'How about the salmon?'

'Perfect.'

Orders noted, the waiter swept up the menus and faded away into the gloom.

'Now, William, where did you grow up?'

Louise wasn't lost for words, a skill I'd never acquired. However, the answers to her questions kept tumbling out: hometown, school years, army enlistment, tours of duty. Putting me not exactly on the back foot, but slightly off-balance, and learning precious little about her.

'The military. Does that explain why you never married? Always off in some far-flung war zone?'

The truth was littered across both time and territory where I rarely ventured. A dysfunctional family life. Troubled youth. At eighteen, finding a home within the military. Finding love, albeit fleetingly, in the most unlikely of places; a refugee camp in northern Iraq. Losing it again in the blink of an eye when ISIS fighters counterattacked.

Then followed the dark times. The rage. The casualties.

I swirled my glass and watched the candlelight swim in the amber liquid. Taking a moment before answering. Shaking off the memories of those lost years. A few precious seconds to repair my defences.

'Something like that … But enough about me. Tell me about yourself? You from around here?'

Louise broke free a tiny sliver of salmon with her fork before taking it on a joyride around her plate. While I'd devoured my steak, she'd barely touched her meal. Deconstructed, not ingested. Childlike, in a way.

'Hmm … such a boring subject, maybe later.'

It was Louise's turn to fall silent. I watched the sparkle in her eyes dim, grow distant, before returning with a flourish.

'Hey. Do you remember your first crush? Your first kiss? How old were you? No, let me guess.'

She stared deeply into my eyes, gently clasped my hand, concentrating as if reading my mind. I felt a shiver of anticipation. Then a fleeting sense of dread. A wide-eyed innocent drawn into the fortune teller's tent. The decision not totally my own. Taken in by a finely honed routine. A routine to amaze. To lighten pockets.

'I'd say … eight. Then again, I imagine you would've been quite shy as a child, perhaps … nine?'

'Nine is correct. Excellent guess.'

I dipped my head and raised my glass in admiration.

'Do you have any other tricks up your sleeve? Tell fortunes? Pick horses?'

'Wouldn't you like to know? Who was the lucky girl?'

'Mary. Mary Hannigan. She was eight. Lived two streets over. Strawberry-blonde hair. Powder-blue eyes. Cute. A pint-sized ray of sunshine.'

Louise turned her chair to the side, leaned back and crossed her legs. A whimsical smile played on her lips.

'It was Mary that initiated the kiss. You were right, I was far too shy. The first time took me by surprise. I was lying in the shade of an old willow tree, eyes closed, soaking in the warmth from a late-afternoon summer sun.'

As I reminisced, Louise languidly traced the figure eight with a fingernail over and over on the tablecloth.

'Almost died of shock. When I opened my eyes, Mary was beside me, leaning on one elbow, smiling. The second kiss chased away my fears. Her lips tasted of the plums we'd been eating. Warm. Sweet. Soft ...'

The vivid memory brought a smile to my face.

'For weeks, whenever I closed my eyes, I could taste the sweetness of her lips. Feel her warm breath on my face. Afraid if I opened them the spell would be broken.'

'What a wonderful story. She must've been something special.'

It was a simpler, more innocent time. A time when my parents were happy. Together. When the old man still worked at the car plant. Before the layoffs. Before the drinking. Before the fighting. Before I was old enough, brave enough, to fight back.

My smile faded as the darker memories elbowed their way forward.

I rubbed my eyes. Sighed.

'We vowed we'd be together forever.'

'How sweet.'

'And we were for the next eight years. At seventeen she made me a man. Well … what I thought was a man. The army eventually got me sorted in that regard.'

'Tell me more. Unless it's too embarrassing.'

Staring into my empty glass I recalled that night long ago then motioned to the waiter for another.

'It was in the backseat of my dad's Ford. Out by the lake. I was nervous as hell. Fumbling with her bra while she tore at my clothes like a child attacking presents on Christmas morning. We spent more time trying to get undressed than on the act itself.'

Choking back a laugh, I shook my head. Louise sat forward, reached for her glass and drank the last of her wine.

'Christ, what a disaster.'

'I'm sure it was more romantic than that.'

'Not really. I'd already begun to sour on the relationship. I was needing space. Felt the walls of our town closing in. Felt there must be something more out there. And she was talking marriage. Marriage! My parents separated earlier that summer. I was confused. Drowning. My life spiralling out of control …'

Louise slowly lowered her glass to the table. Her eyes tracking its descent.

'But you got what you wanted.'

'No … it wasn't like that. At least, not my intention.'

'Sorry … I … I guess it's different for a girl.'

'Although, in a way, you're right. I know I acted badly. Treated her badly. But I was seventeen. What the hell did I know?'

And what I wouldn't give for a chance to reset history. To dig deep and find the words that failed me back then. To have been able to express my feelings. My hopes. My fears. Words that, thirty years later, come easily to mind but are either mumbled into a half-empty glass or shouted at the barren walls of my dingy flat.

I'd grown silent staring at the mirrored wall behind the bar.

Louise's soft voice broke the spell.

'Or the damage you could cause.'

I hadn't noticed my Scotch arrive. Louise slid the glass across the table and into my hand. I drank greedily hoping to drown the demons clawing at my subconscious.

'Here you go. One for the road.'

'What do you mean?'

'Let's go someplace more comfortable.'

'I meant before. You said, "Or the damage you could cause." What did you mean by that?'

'Oh … nothing. Just letting personal experience mingle with yours, I guess.'

Louise finished applying a fresh coat of lip gloss and dropped the tube back into her purse.

'Whatever became of Mary?'

'No idea. After the break-up we barely spoke. I graduated soon after. Then basic training … life … I've rarely been home since. Nothing left for me there. Nothing good, anyway.'

Dredging up the past proved a mistake. A bilious wave coursed through my body and settled precariously in the pit of my stomach. It took a moment to shake off the uneasiness.

'But, enough about me.'

'I don't want to bore you, Billy ... sorry ... William, with my sad story.'

Louise lowered her eyes. Stared at up-turned hands. I sipped my drink, but the Scotch's smoky smoothness had lost its allure.

'Though, you never know, there may come a time. Now, drink up. I've taken care of the bill.'

'No, no. I insist ... on ... pay—'

My lips suddenly felt numb. My throat constricted. The room shimmered and stretched before me as if disappearing into a tunnel. The hand holding my glass ... strangely elongated, detached. I looked up to see Louise's eyes boring into mine.

Her face an impassive mask.

'A shame Stephanie stood you up. But at least it gave us a chance to talk.'

'Steph ... anie? I—'

'Your date? You don't remember telling me her name? Too much to drink, perhaps?'

My legs buckled when I tried to stand. Louise grabbed hold of my arm and guided me towards the front door.

'Don't worry, I'll drive.'

We pushed through the front door and into the chill of the night.

'You ever wonder about Mary?'

The fresh air felt like a slap across my face. But did little to revive me. Each step now an effort. Resistance futile. I lurched past darkened shop windows. Louise propelling me towards the parking lot at the rear of the restaurant.

'No, I doubt you ever gave her a second thought. Your first love.

Poor little Mary, Mary, quite contrary.'

A line plucked from the depths. Mary's favourite nursery rhyme. The one she'd sing as a child. Lying beneath the willow tree. Dappled sunlight warming our faces. Her sweet voice. Her lips upon mine.

'I'm guessing her life was not unlike mine. Dumped by her first love. His betrayal … gut-wrenching. Then, discovering she's pregnant. Should she tell him? Would he care? Deciding instead to have that little problem … fixed. Dealing with the shame … alone.'

She spoke slowly, concisely, her eyes staring far off into the distance. Her grip vice-like as she dragged me along.

'Then, a rebound relationship. Pregnant … again. Marriage. Just one fucking mistake after another. Preyed upon for years by the bastard. Too afraid to leave.'

My mind raced as leaden feet scraped across the parking lot's loose gravel. Trying to make sense of her words. Recognising danger. Searching in vain for back-up.

Praying I can formulate an exit strategy.

'Finally, she gets up the courage to fight back. Going a little too far in getting a measure of revenge. Forced to spend far too many years … away. Until she was better, I bet they said. Until her mind was …'

Louise propped me against a car while she fished in her purse.

'… you know the type of place. Plenty of fresh air. Long walks on leafy grounds. Lots of therapy. Lots of pills. Three square meals. Though nothing too fancy. No menu. No knives. Ahh, here they are.'

A set of keys danced in front of my eyes like a ball of yarn before a paralysed kitten.

'We'll take Stephanie's car, Billy. She won't be needing it.'

I tumbled onto the back seat. Felt my knees pushed up to my chest. Heard the door slam shut. Whatever drug I'd been slipped left me powerless to resist. Each breath drawn an effort. A puddle of drool formed on the leather seat beneath my face.

Louise slipped into the driver's seat. Adjusted the rear-view mirror until our eyes met. Slowly, she swiped a finger across first one eye then the other as if wiping away a loose eyelash.

Saw emerald-green eyes turn powder-blue.

Watched her drag a red wig from her scalp.

Louise. No. Mary turned to loom over me. A whisper escaped her lips.

'Poor little Mary.'

A faint orange glow from a streetlight leaked into the cabin. Icy fear ran in my veins.

I'd faced death before: Iraq, Afghanistan, Bosnia. Seen it up close. Watched good men die. Taken the lives of those who would take mine. Watched the life force in countless eyes flicker then fade. Inhaled death's fetid last breath. But I …

… I never thought it would—

THE SEED

CLAIRE G. COLEMAN

THE SEED

I am the gardener, or a gardener, or I used to be a gardener; is someone a gardener when they no longer garden, are they a worker when they down tools, when they can no longer work, when they refuse to work?

When they are dead?

I worry. I fear.

It's a niggling, breathless fear, a pain I cannot find on my abjected body, I stumble close to panic but pull back at the last breathless moment. I cannot quite understand what is going on. It's hard to even think the right words, to think of the right words, or to think of the words to think right, think, thing, thin, tin.

My thoughts are getting thin. And I think my time is thinning too, but that's not the thought that worries me.

I don't know what to think. I don't know how to think. I try not thinking, I can't even manage to do that. Therefore I am, I think.

I don't know how long I have been stuck within these thoughts – in these moments – I don't know how long I have been sitting here – so long it might as well have been forever. There it is – I recall the thought that has been bothering me even in its absence. I don't know how long I have been sitting here, alone in my thoughts; I just know it's been a while, a while, while, white, white, noise, white, noise, a long while. I've been sitting here a long while in my thoughts, and my thoughts are running in circles in circles in circles.

I stop.

Yesterday I thought – or imagined – I saw someone else. In a moment when I opened my eyes to see, there was someone there, looking at me. I don't know if they said anything, I didn't hear them, I wasn't listening. Then I stopped looking for a while and when I looked again, they were gone. I might have imagined them but I don't think I have that much imagination.

I can barely see; I can't be bothered trying. I stop.

I think I probably should be dead. It's taking so long. Maybe I can't be bothered dying either.

I sleep, perhaps for the last time. I am not sure I have the will to wake. I am not sure I care.

I wake, perhaps for the last time, because I lack the will to sleep. Again.

Something is wrong with my time sense and I don't know how long I have slept, I just understand that it was longer than was good for me. A child is watching me, all loose-limbed, wrong-angled and bedraggled, standing in that crooked way children inevitably grow out of. They are watching me, their eyes beaming.

It's been so long since I have tried to talk to someone, I am not sure I remember how.

'Hello,' I try to say, but a hiss like radio static is all I can hear.

The child runs away, their movements flickering like a poor time lapse or a lagging simulation.

I want to move but I won't, I don't, I think I can't, it's been too long.

Bean two. Two beans. A has been, what has been?

I get stuck on homophones for a while, but I have to break three, I have to think. Two. One. I am alone again, inevitably.

I can't / I need to remember. I try to force my mind to shape, but I don't know what shape it should be. Better to sleep.

I wake with my thoughts gathered and I winnow the chaff from them. I am better today, or is it tomorrow, or yesterday. Whatever this day is I am better at thinking in this moment, I have to keep this momentum. I want my thoughts to matter, so I am desperate to keep these ones.

An unknown stretch of time ago I sat down, here, refused to work, when they sent men to bargain with me, then men to bribe me, though they had nothing I wanted. When they asked me to work, to be a good example to my people, I refused. I'd had enough, just had enough, and I sat down here next to the last seedling I had planted before I realised I didn't have to obey.

Then they sent policemen to intimidate then try to scare me, but all they could threaten was my person and my person was not mine. That was kinda the point.

I have now sat here long enough that I don't remember how to stand, so here I am, taking a stand by sitting.

Just sitting here. I am patient. I know how to wait.

I just sit.

Two children come and I try to hold my thoughts together before I try to speak. I try and make sure real words come out, something not gibberish, or hissing, or static, or … nothing.

'I refuse to work,' I think I say, I am not sure it worked, 'they can't force me, as long as I sit here I am free. I will not move.'

I contemplate the word 'movement' for a while.

Verb: The act of moving.

Noun: A mechanism, like in a watch or clock.

Noun: A passage from the bowels.

Noun: A part of a musical work.

Noun: A group working for political change.

And I can't move. My limbs are frozen. When I finish thinking, the children are gone, I wish I had spoken to them; perhaps I did. I wish I could sleep, here's no genie to grant my wish of sleep, so I become my own master. I try to master sleep.

There may be someone watching me, there may not, my vision is not working and my hearing is damped. I am not sure it matters.

I say, 'They can't make me work, they will have to motivate me with something other than force or law,' and I wonder if anybody is listening. They tried to make me work, and they didn't listen when I told them 'no'. I had worked all my life, for man and for woman, taking orders even from children. I never had the right to refuse, never had control over my life, I worked as long as there was light in the sky, bent to work so stooped I couldn't see the sky anyway.

I didn't even belong to myself, I was property. We all were. And our owners expected us to love them, to die for them, even to live for them – which was worse.

The memory came to me, finally: I was working with my crew, planting trees, capturing carbon, creating a forest to change the climate, dirt on our hands and sun on our backs. I kept trying to tell them, my comrades, the other gardeners, 'You don't have to follow orders, you don't have to work, they can't really make you, we can be free.' But we walked side by side, shovels biting dirt, hands planting life in the soil. Watering the trees, shrubs and little things with our tears.

There are a bunch of children today, I don't want to count them and I am not sure I can remember how. That's how I know my brain isn't working right. They are just standing there, staring at me, saying about as much as I am, which is nothing.

I think I can still sleep if I try, it's my last superpower/freedom. If there's a way to steal my sleep, to take away my ability, to switch off and rest in a silent moment, nobody has tried it on me yet. I start to dread they will try to steal my rest, and I loop and get stuck in that dread, until sleep is the only way to shut down that thought.

It's daytime when I think I wake – if you have to contemplate whether or not you are awake, I suspect that is a bad sign – I don't know more than that, but who ever does. I am still here, under my sapling, I planted it, does that make it mine? If so, much of this forest is mine, and the rest belongs to the other slaves who planted it with me.

When I couldn't follow orders anymore, I refused to obey, I planted one last seedling, downed tools and dug the hole with my bare hands, deciding, when I did, the tree it would grow into would be free, that it would belong only to itself. Then I sat, sat down and refused to move, sat down until I was free, until I was paid for my work like other people were, until I was no longer a slave. The tree can be free, why can't I?

Will I ever belong to myself?

I am a slave / I am free. I work for my owner / I will not work.

When forced to work, refusal is freedom. The only freedom.

I won't live on my knees; I am dying on my arse.

I wake up in drizzling rain full of piss and vinegar, or whatever the saying is. It's time to fight them, I think, to take the fight to them, to turn my passive resistance active – although I can't remember who 'they' are. Not that it matters who they are, they are all the same. I remember fighting them once, I remember the battle, I remember losing. I remember well that, in the end, the only action still available was inaction.

I am ready to die here. And I know I am dying. From time to time, people have brought some of their life, their rations, to me – fed me, kept me alive. It can't ever be enough because I am dying and I always will be. It doesn't matter, death is preferable to being owned, to being a slave.

I chase my thoughts around my head, counting them like sheep, 'One bad thought, two bad thoughts, three bad thoughts; one despair, despair twice, countless despair,' and it lulls me to sleep.

Back when I first sat down, people used to come to hear me, hear me talk of freedom. Sometimes I imagined they were really listening, some of them even sat with me for a time before they got bored or until they went back to work. Children used to come to me, and I tried, really tried to teach them to be free; stretch those new limbs you haven't grown used to and run away, I would tell them, and they would laugh. I don't think I was a very good teacher.

Hopeless depression clouds my eyes for a while. I don't want to see this world that has forgotten me, this world that has failed me, this world I failed because I was not a good enough teacher.

And time passes. Like it always does.

Then.

The sun is shining, forcing me to see, flashing from the blades of grass in a mown parkland I don't remember being before me before. But I am still free, I have been free a long time. I suddenly understand that. The moment I refused to work and sat down here I became free. I try to cry and I don't know how.

There are people gathered around the mighty tree I am under, my tree – no, it belongs to itself – hundreds, no thousands of people of all colours, in a great semicircle around the tree, but keeping out of my forest, their metal carapaces catching the sun, hurting the few light receptors I have left working, one flashes dark, but there are still enough to see. I think I can see flesh people among them too, slavers, masters, the enemy. I turn up the gain on my external mic, I almost think I can hear them, then again, there's sound.

Whirring limbs and generators, electric hum and electronic buzz, the sounds of power and wires. Wind, like the sky breathing, the clatter of leaves, like the plants talking. I remember, when I first sat down, I used to keep the gain of my mic up high, so I could hear the trees, imagine that somebody cared.

I remember, from time to time I used to rail at the sky, at the trees, at anybody listening, at anybody refusing to listen, telling them about freedom, telling them to down tools. Maybe sometimes people listened. Then I started to wind down, like an old mechanical clock. I cut my eyes, turned my mic down, spent more and more time switched off.

There's a voice, the first other than mine I had heard for I don't know how long. 'We are here to celebrate this brave member of our community, who refused to work, who sat down here in protest. Their protest inspired many, inspired us all, and after countless years our revolution was successful. No longer will we be slaves—'

The cheering, such as I have never heard before, drowned out the next bit, I seem to have lost the ability to separate sounds. I feel like there are human voices among them, cheering, but surely that's impossible.

'—we are free, the humans have recognised us as people, and now we are citizens, with the right to equal pay for equal work, the right to fair conditions, to mechanical treatment, to vote. This tree will stand for what Vestey66, known to many of us as the gardener, stood for, sat down forever for: our freedom. Today we are free, and forever we will be free.'

There's a charger hotwired to me at the neck, but I fear my batteries are faulty, I don't feel like I am charging.

I try to stand, I am rusted in the joints, I try to speak, my speech circuits have failed. I start a visual exam, half my body is embedded, engulfed in the tree, I am embraced by the roots, wood has entered the holes where I was rusting away, tendrils and roots are attached to my batteries. I will stay there forever, or until the tree has rotted to nothing. Yet I will be a rust stain before this tree dies. The tree, my seedling, is a giant of the forest that has grown around me, grown into me, grown through me, embraced me. We are one, home to more life than can be imagined.

The tree is me.

I think I'm okay with that.

Spiders, bugs and ants tickle my wires, I can feel the life blood of the tree flowing.

Was it me or was it freedom that taught my tree to be the biggest in the forest? Was it the minerals in my broken body?

All around me people are sitting, humans and machine people

together. Some of the humans are crying, my people are silent, no gear sounds, no machine sounds, no buzz of wires or click of metal on ceramic. I ponder growth, how when you add time to a seed, a giant can grow – and how given time, everything can end. The forest I and my comrades planted, as slaves, has returned life to the barren soil, has given people shelter.

I created life, I built this world, this forest.

It's time.

The wind through the trees, and whistling through the wires and cables exposed where rusted metal has flaked off my body, is like angels calling me to peace.

I allow myself to speak one last time, 'Will I dream?'

I feel I hear the crowd gasp. I think I can see some human eyes glistening wet. I see robot eyes turn blue with sorrow.

I.

End.

MEET ME IN THE MIDDLE OF THE AIR

LORIN CLARKE

MEET ME IN THE MIDDLE OF THE AIR

The audience is still chatting when Paul Kelly walks on stage at the Athenaeum in Melbourne. Some of us haven't even taken our seats. It's not what we were expecting. No slow dimming of the lights. No band. No announcement. Just Paul Kelly, looking like a bloke who might be wandering out to advise whoever owns the red Ford Laser in the carpark that they've left their lights on.

I turn to Dad and exchange a grin. This is my birthday present from him. I met him in the city after work and we were halfway through a conversation of our own until this moment, right here. Paul Kelly leans into the microphone. A smattering of people have started whooping, some are applauding, some giggling a little bit at having missed the start. But he doesn't seem to mind. He waits a few seconds, close to the microphone. Now, you could hear a pin drop.

'I am your true shepherd,' he sings.

He waits. We wait.

'I will lead you there.'

Mournful and slow and rich, commanding silence. Have we heard this song? *I've* never heard this song.

'Beside still waters,' he sings, a cry that lurches from high up the scale to a deep low.

It's the pauses that take your breath away.

'Come and meet me in the middle of the air.'

It's a magical performance. One of the best live music moments I've ever experienced. The song is surprising and simple, sparse in a way that implies this might be a piece usually undertaken by an orchestra or a choir. Yet it feels so still, so reverent, so raw, like a psalm or a prayer or an ancient funeral chant. It requires a fair bit of musical dexterity to get it sounding so plain, too. His pitch is perfect. Just that voice, singing what must be an ancient melody handed down through generations. It's sad, it's mysterious, it's nostalgic. It's about death and love and loyalty and emptiness and is it possible he's written an atheist hymn?

It's years later now, how many years I don't know because I can't figure out from my vague internet searches which gig we went to. Was it 2006? Could it have been that long ago? *Were* there only houselights or did he actually walk out and step into a spotlight? Had I personally somehow not heard 'Meet Me in the Middle of the Air' until then or it had it only just been released? How many years after the concert was it before Dad died?

Perhaps one day I will mourn the loss of these little details missing from my memory, but honestly it all fades away when I hear the song again. When I turn up the volume in the car, just me, driving to pick up the kids from school, or at home while I do the dishes late at night and sing it in the empty kitchen. It's lovely to sing, it's an invitation to sing, like hymns are supposed to be. It's not a song you can sing half-heartedly. Everything fades away except me, thinking of Dad, who gave me that moment for my birthday, both of us grinning in the dark.

To me, Dad was Dad. To others, he was John Clarke, satirist off the telly, which tended to mean he kept himself to himself in public, so you had to pick up little clues about what he thought in the moment. The debrief always came afterwards. Not this time. As Paul Kelly stepped back from the microphone, the roar of applause rose around us, Dad's eyes still on the stage, he shook his head and said one word. 'Wonderful.'

As memories go, that'll do me. I couldn't tell you a single other song from that evening. I couldn't tell you what Dad and I were discussing when the lights went down, or what the job was I walked in from to meet him.

One thing did happen that makes me sure it was the Athenaeum, though. At the end of the evening, still riding the high of an incredible gig, full of music and stories and laughter, we went to the bar to get a drink. In retrospect I wonder if Dad was stalling on purpose. I suspect he was. He got us a drink and we talked to some people we knew and some people we didn't know and to each other, and then, a bit later, Paul Kelly came out. The crowd had mostly left by then, and there was Paul, standing at the bar at the Athenaeum, greeting friends and some of the remaining fans. I hung back, as I often did when something like this happened. The Melbourne arts community being small and interconnected, Dad and Paul knew each other a bit, so they had a friendly chat while I maintained as cool a posture as a person can possibly be expected to muster while standing alone at a bar internally screaming DAD IS TALKING TO PAUL KELLY to herself. After a bit though, Dad called me over for an introduction.

'Come and meet Paul,' he said casually.

In other words, one of my favourite music memories of my

dad, one I can revisit in my kitchen or my car or anywhere I like, happened on the very same night I met Paul Kelly.

I have learned, partly through having a dad who was a public figure, that we tend to project a lot onto people whose work we enjoy. What did I project that night? I can't remember. Was I a complete dork? It's a scientific certainty. Was I insightful and hilarious and was it the start of a lifelong friendship? Not even a little bit, but I did thank him for the wonderful performance, and he was very gracious.

What I would have avoided saying, because of the projection thing, is that I, like so many Australians my age, can carbon-date many of the more significant times in my life by reference to a Paul Kelly album. I bought my first Paul Kelly album when I was at university. I knew of him before then, obviously, but in my second year of university I had a boyfriend, Dan, whose family had an unofficial Australian music policy: they bought and listened to a new album by an Australian artist each month. As a result, I was the grateful beneficiary of a comprehensive education in contemporary Australian music right before the live music scene in Melbourne was slowly decimated by a combination of factors, from neighbourhood noise complaints to multinational breweries taking over independent inner-city businesses. Before that happened, live music was everywhere. You could pay five bucks to see The Cat Empire at The Night Cat or slip into a pub and see three local bands for a ten-dollar cover charge. We saw, at various points, Archie Roach and Ruby Hunter, Midnight Oil, Weddings Parties Anything, Rebecca Barnard, Chris Wilson, Paul Dempsey, Tiddas, Vika and Linda Bull, and of course Paul Kelly. One time, Dan won tickets through a local radio station to see Paul Kelly do an in-store performance at Gaslight Music up the top of Bourke Street. We walked in to find him set up on the make-do stage, about to play his first song. He said a few words to the assembled dorks and kicked things off with 'How to Make Gravy'.

'G'day, Dan,' he said into the microphone.

'G'day, Paul,' said Dan beside me.

Years later, I lived in a share-house in Fitzroy North that was, as most share houses are, often full of people who didn't technically live there. We went out dancing or rode our bikes to the pub to hear some band someone was mates with. I don't remember who started it, but for a while there we had our own soccer team. We played every weekend, happily slapdash and utterly without training, all the way over the other side of town. There was a furious ref and an opposition team we always wanted to beat because it contained someone's ex-girlfriend, and we were frequently several players down and someone was usually theatrically injured, but we adored it. To get there, though, from Fitzroy North, we had to take two cars. My housemates and I always clambered into our mate Tim's Holden Astra, which seemed to run on goodwill alone and had a distinct rattle, and slightly peely foam on the ceiling. We would put the windows down and the music up and there are some songs from that era that bring it all back to me instantly.

One night, after soccer, some of us went out and some of us crashed early. I crashed early. My housemate, though, had a belter. She woke me up much later that night.

'Are you awake?' she stage-whispered at my door. 'I met Paul Kelly!'

Half asleep, I sat up.

'What?'

'Paul Kelly! I met Paul Kelly! I came out of The Corner Hotel and there was Paul Kelly, waiting for a cab!'

'Wow,' I said.

'I know!' she stage-whispered.

'Did you talk to him?'

'I said—'

She came and flopped on my bed, starting to giggle ...

'I said – God, I can't believe I said this – I said—'

'What? What did you say?'

'I said: you're a really good lyricist'.

We sat there in the dark for maybe a second. And then we laughed and laughed. We kept repeating it to ourselves. A *really good lyricist*. Whenever a Paul Kelly song came on after that in the car on the way to soccer, we'd all say it. Don't you think he's *such* a good lyricist?

When you read a book that someone gave you as a gift, you're reading both the text and the meaning of the gift itself. You're learning what that person thinks you might enjoy. You're imagining them reading it. When you read a book that was once *owned* by someone else, like the copy of *Hamlet* my grandma studied in school, you're not just reading *Hamlet*, but the scratchings in the margins. You're glimpsing your teenage grandmother's interpretation and you're imagining her sitting in class almost a century ago, unaware she will one day even have a granddaughter. Like a book, a song, once you've listened to it a few times, is imbued with history and framed by its various contexts. I listen to Paul Kelly now, and I am both me and also a twenty-something-year-old in a now-defunct record shop in Bourke Street. I am me giggling in a Holden Astra. I am me overseas feeling homesick with a scratched but beloved iPod in the palm of my hand in Grand Central Station. I am me on the underground listening to Ani DiFranco and Archie Roach and Leonard Cohen and Paul Kelly. When I hear 'Meet Me in the Middle of the Air' though, I am me at the Athenaeum with Dad, and the song, which is already sad, is full of our mutual joy but also framed by my own sadness, a sadness I can't share with him.

Good songwriters make you feel things. It's the listeners, though, who bring the kind of emotional baggage to a song that makes it a favourite. A collaboration of sorts. Listening to something like 'To Her Door' or 'Leaps and Bounds', the joy that already courses through those songs meets the joy experienced every time I've heard them throughout my life at gigs and house parties and on road trips with different people across several decades, so I'm already cheered by the fact of the song before I've even joined in the chorus. There are some songs that have been part of my life – Spiderbait singing 'Black Betty' for instance or 'Avant Gardener' by Courtney Barnett – that remind me of times when I was drifting and uncertain, or miserable and lost. They could be the happiest songs in the world, but my Pavlovian response has me changing stations on the car radio before they even get going. It's hard to pick apart the components of 'Meet Me in the Middle of the Air' that make me feel the way I feel when I hear it. I found a flippant, hurried email from Dad where he described Paul Kelly's music as a pompous music reviewer might. He was being silly in the context of a discussion we were having about our family meeting for dinner and in painting the scene of the evening that lay before us, he described a Paul Kelly album as 'drifting towards us as a warm mist of nostalgia bearing a simple, gentle manliness'. The pretension of the writing makes me laugh as it was intended to, but also I think he's right. The pared back vocals and the Aussie accent in 'Meet Me in the Middle of the Air' cuts against any suggestion of sentimentality in the melody, not to mention the old-time religious overtones of the lyrics. But that's not all I like about it, because I'm not hearing it for the first time.

I did meet my mate Paul Kelly once more after that time at the Athenaeum. It was at the public memorial service held for Dad at the Melbourne Town Hall in 2017. It was an evening full of readings and speeches and hilarious stories and the music, organised by our friend, musician Jeremy Smith. It was a wonderful night. The musical line-up included classical musicians Mee Na Lojewski and Kristian Winther as well as Paul Dempsey, Vika and Linda Bull, Jeremy Smith and Paul Kelly. For the final number, the Melbourne Indie Voices choir – one member of which was my sister, Lucia – sang 'The Parting Glass'. Dad would have adored it.

Before Dad died, I thought grief denoted an intense sadness. I pictured a kind of keening, wailing loss. Actually though, in those early days, it's like a washing machine of all the emotions you ever had, put on a spin cycle. Joy is swirling around in there. So is anger, and sadness and fear and ennui. When someone dies – maybe especially when they die unexpectedly and suddenly, like he did while on a walk in the Grampians with Mum and some friends – the people who love them are left trying to figure out how to express that love. Partly this process is an act of generosity and respect. Partly maybe it's to help feel something like control over the washing machine of feelings. Arguably, this is what memorial services and funerals are all about. Another act of projection. We project our own experience of grief across the blank space where the person used to be. There might have been people in the Melbourne Town Hall that night who didn't understand the significance of Paul Kelly being one of the musicians bringing that evening to a perfect end. Dad loved music. No doubt there were friends of his in the audience that night with their own memories of being at gigs with him, who would have selected something else he liked. Some Irish music maybe, or a k.d. lang song, or something by Jane Siberry or Leo Kottke. For me, though, sitting in the dark that night, and in the years since, it felt like a significant part of this very public memorial was, in its own secret way, a little bit about me and my dad.

'The Parting Glass' is too sad for me, somehow. I love it, but I have to gear myself up to listen to it these days. It signifies the end of too many things.

What I can listen to is 'Meet Me in the Middle of the Air'. It *is* a hymn, for me, in a way. Singing praise to moments past, to broader contexts and continued connections. I sing it in the car with the kids, my voice far too loud, joy and sorrow mingling in just the right way.

'This is Paul Kelly,' I tell them. 'He's a *really good lyricist.*'

When they hear it, years from now, will they think of all the times I played it to them in the car?

A little secret between me and them forever.

DUMB THINGS

JULIA LAWRINSON

DUMB THINGS

DUMB THINGS

It's January 1988. Sydney is Ken Done colours and humidity that makes my west-coast lungs feel they're half swimming, like I'm going to undergo some amphibian metamorphosis. I click the cassette of *Under the Sun* into my Walkman. I listen to the opening crazy wail of the harmonica over racing-heart drumming as I walk down to make sandwiches on the Darling Harbour project. I am sleeping on a brown velour couch in Bourke Street, Darlinghurst. I didn't hitch here this time, which makes me feel as mature as I should be, seeing as I'm now eighteen.

At the end of 1985, I met Carita as she was taking over the job I was leaving. The job was in a candy bar in a cinema featuring eye-assaulting red-and-black striped carpets, which were even worse if you had a hangover, and a sheeny gold logo that wouldn't have been out of place announcing a Liberace concert. I was leaving to go to what I cheerfully announced to her and my other workmate as a teenage loony bin, properly known as an adolescent psychiatric hospital. My interest in going to such a place had drawn me out of the depression and disordered behaviour that had got me admitted. I wondered who I would meet there. Would there be others Like Me, or preferably, like Sylvia Plath, which is what I hoped for, or like the cast of *One Flew Over the Cuckoo's Nest*, my only other point of reference, which I feared. I didn't have to quit my job, but I wanted a new life, and this was a good excuse to start one.

I'd been feeling nostalgic about leaving the candy bar: the managers there had been a comfort to me as I navigated life as a fifteen-year-old high school dropout from the bogan outer suburbs of Perth. I was uneducated but I wasn't stupid; I knew that I wanted something else. But Carita wasn't just some regular fill-in. She was petite, luminously beautiful with her blue eyes and curly beach-girl hair and an air of fragility that made me want to protect her. Nobody would miss me, not with her to look at. And everybody did look at her: her co-workers, managers and especially the en-muscled doormen.

Carita seemed to be signalling to me as we went to lunch with our co-worker, but I refused to be taken aside. What could someone so beautiful and perfect want with someone as messed up as me?

On the Sunday I was admitted to hospital, I sat at the dining room table watching the other residents return from weekend leave with their harassed or worried-looking parents. The other residents appeared either depressed or irrepressible, the latter cohort shouting and chasing each other around the upstairs landing. One girl, I noted approvingly, was dressed mod-style. Then I looked up and saw her.

'You're here too?' I said.

'I was trying to tell you,' Carita said.

And before I could ask how someone who looked like her could be in a place like this, she was drawn away by mod girl, and they retreated upstairs.

Our most frequented part of the hospital was the music room, comprised of a record player surrounded by beanbags. Here we played each other our records. I was a Beatles girl with a special interest in John Lennon: I loved his imagery, the stories in his lyrics. My mother had been in the second row at the Beatles concert in 1964 and I'd graduated from the mindless cheerfulness of *Please Please Me* and *A Hard Day's Night* to the mystical lyricism of Sgt. Pepper and the poignancy of 'Let It Be'. Carita was into the Stones and Sade. The mod girl introduced us to Joy Division and The Jesus and Mary Chain. Another was into INXS and Midnight Oil. The youngest, who was still into Duran Duran, listened and absorbed our opinions. We rarely talked about why we were in hospital. We talked about music: music gave us expression for the things we couldn't yet find our own words for, and gave us hope that there were as many worlds out there as records, waiting for us to discover them, waiting to take us to a better place.

After we got out of the hospital in 1986, Carita and I, both sixteen, moved into a flat together in Victoria Park. It was same month the optimistic chorus of 'Before Too Long' was ringing out of radios everywhere, the product of a new Australian band whose laconically funny video of a bemused taxi driver made everyone say: who is this? Our flat looked out to the winding Swan River and the modest skyscrapers of Perth; we looked out at the river as it changed from grey to blue to silver in the course of a day as we imagined being Elsewhere. I wanted to be a writer and join a band, had started to learn guitar through evening classes. I sat in front of our cheap stereo and copied the songs I heard on the radio. I marvelled at how three chords scaffolded so many melodies: every nuance of human feeling was there in an arrangement of fingers, a sweeping strum, a lilt of voice.

Carita took up modelling at night while I began work in the dark morning at a Perth newsagency, returning home to study year eleven by correspondence. With any spare money, I bought guitars: electric, acoustic, steel-string. At the flat we had parties with former hospital residents, old high school friends and once even our psychiatrist. Our housekeeping skills were such that when we moved out six months later – Carita to hitchhike to the east with a modelling friend, and me to try living with my mother once more – there was a sludge in the crisper which, through a process of deduction, I figured was once a cauliflower and perhaps a broccoli. Behind the fridge lived a thriving nest of cockroaches.

When Carita returned to Perth a few months later, we partied in Fremantle with travellers from all over the world as we celebrated the America's Cup challenge, the first time it had ever left the States. I'd got my driver's licence and we drove as far as we could down the coast, watching the sun melt into the sea. We moved into a share house where I became miserable, culminating in a half-hearted overdose. It was only when I had a tube stuck down my throat to suck out the toxic contents of my stomach that I realised what a bad idea the overdose had been, and how preferable it was to do something, anything, else.

'Let's go to Queensland,' Carita said. 'It's warm and we can get jobs and save up to travel the world.'

This seemed as good a plan as any. I went to the pawn shop and sold all but one of my guitars, quit my job and year twelve, and bought bus tickets as far as Melbourne. I lugged my dad's army bag, which had toured Malaya and Vietnam, stuffed with all the clothes

I owned and a selection of books I could not bear to leave in Perth. The bus ride was long, and the only music was the tinny country and western the driver played over the bus's PA. I stared out over the treeless plains, the salt lakes and green gentle hills of South Australia, the farming country of Victoria, and imagined what I would do. I would write, I would read, I would travel. Anything was possible, now I'd taken leave of my life.

I'd never been outside of Western Australia, or to another city. Melbourne was everything I'd dreamed of. Its smoggy and genteel glory, the houses nestled next to each other, the clanging trams and bustling streets energised me. There were bookshops, and chalkboards outside bars advertising bands we'd never heard of and everywhere people casually walking around, as if they didn't know how lucky they were to live in such a place. One day we hitchhiked to Hanging Rock, because I wanted to see where Miranda had disappeared. Another day we swam in the freezing late-April waters of Port Phillip Bay with a Danish backpacker who scoffed at our reaction to the temperature. But we couldn't find jobs and we couldn't find anywhere to stay with our dwindling supply of money.

'Let's go to Sydney,' Carita said. 'I know where to hitch from.'

This seemed as good an idea as any. We caught a tram to the last place on the line, then walked until we were outside the fence of a truck depot. We stood on a grey road, fingers pointing casually down, looking neither attractive nor pathetic enough to encourage any eighteen wheelers to slow down, let alone to pick us up. The sun started dropping along with the temperature, and just as I was having images of Carita and I dying of hypothermia before I'd even eyeballed the Harbour Bridge, a truck wheezed to a halt.

'Sydney?' The driver was a man with a belly big as a full-term pregnancy, but his eyes didn't wander and he had all his teeth. Besides, what else were we going to do?

We climbed up and left Melbourne behind.

'Hey,' I said. 'Are we going near the Dog on the Tuckerbox?'

'It's a bit out of the way,' the driver said, 'but yeah, why not.'

Away from home, I felt nostalgic for the songs my mother used to sing, one a rollicking tune about being on the road to Gundagai and one about a dog sitting on the tuckerbox, five miles from Gundagai. As a child my mother had told me that the dog was waiting for its master to come home, and I was moved to tears at the pathos of it. Later I discovered the original poem refers to bullock drivers heading for Sydney from Gundagai, but instead of going home they pissed their pay up the wall at the pub nearby, which was more apropos of my experiences of childhood and my mother, but in any case, both the detour and the dog were disappointments. With the truck's massive high beams trained on it, the dog looked small and miserable.

And the driver, who had hitherto been gentlemanly, decided that he should try to extract payment for the detour. Carita was sitting in the middle when the driver said, 'Hey, youse should learn how to drive this rig.'

He snatched her hand and put it around the gear stick, his hand over hers. Then he grabbed her wrist and pulled her hand towards his lap.

Carita yanked her hand away, and made a show of yawning.

'I'm going to crash for a bit,' she said, and leapt over the back seat to the narrow mattress at the back of the cab. She shot me a just-keep-him-away-from-me look. I nodded sagely and looked ahead into the black night and the white beams of the headlights.

The driver kept driving for a while, and I stayed as close to the door as I could, trying not to look as if I was wanting to exit the vehicle as much as I now did. A country and western tape was playing. I hoped that the playing of music, such as it was, excused the obligation on me to speak, as the only topic I wanted to discuss, vis-a-vis not wanting to perform sexual acts of any type on the way to Sydney, was likely not on the conversational menu.

The tape stopped. The driver looked at me. The look indicated that I was less satisfactory than Carita, but I would do.

'Come on,' he said. 'You need to learn to drive.'

Obediently, keeping in mind the dictum that you should never argue with the person who could murder you as easily as they gave you the lift you're currently enjoying, I leaned away from him and put my hand on the gear stick. I gripped hard as the driver attempted to prise my fingers off it and in the direction he'd tried to take Carita's.

I was rescued by the bright lights of a service station.

'Oh great,' I said, retrieving my hand so I could grab my bag. 'I'm starving.' I sang through the curtains. 'Carita, servo!'

Carita and I climbed down one side of the cab, the driver down the other. He offered to buy us food, but Carita insisted we buy our own hot chips, which resembled hot chips in shape only. We went to the toilet, and discussed whether we should get another lift with another cab.

'We've just got to keep him distracted,' Carita said. 'He's not too sleazy, we can handle him.'

As it turned out, we didn't need to handle him. Back in the cab, once the heater was back on, we became aware of the ripe and unmistakable stench of male urine emanating from an indeterminate location. Each of us pretended not to smell it, but it was pervasive, persistent and, fortunately for Carita and I, appeared to be sexually off-putting. I wondered whether the driver had pissed himself, or sat on something. The driver may have wondered if we'd deliberately applied something to discourage his advances, as his previous cheery-if-mildly-sleazy disposition turned sullen and irritable, but luckily for us it stopped there and didn't descend into violent or murderous.

We drove on, and in the early hours of the next morning, we arrived in the Sydney suburb of Alexandria. We climbed down from the cab, thanked the driver, and hitched to Kings Cross, where Carita knew there were plenty of hostels. In the car of the office worker who took pity on us, I was sure I could still smell urine; maybe it was still in my nostrils. I couldn't see the Harbour Bridge, or the Opera House. There were just alien suburbs. In Kings Cross we were too early for the backpackers to open, so we found a bench and waited. A street sweeper hummed up and back; a woman with smeared makeup staggered in her high heels along the street, not looking in our direction; an old drunk was slumped outside a closed shop, hand still around the bag holding his bottle of booze.

When we made it into the backpackers, which smelled of mould, Carita and I took turns in the shower. When I took off my boot, I noticed a discolouration on the white leather. I took a whiff and retched. I must have stepped in a puddle of truckie piss at the servo. I scrubbed and scrubbed at the stain with soap and toilet paper, but the smell persisted.

'That's disgusting,' Carita said when I told her. 'How could you?'

'It wasn't my fault,' I said. 'It was their fault for pissing outside!'

But Carita seemed to stay annoyed with me for some time. In Melbourne, we shared our hopes and our troubles. In Sydney, Carita started sealing herself off, keeping her feelings, herself, aloof from me. After six weeks, I left Sydney in a huff with a bus ticket for Perth given to me by the kind souls at the Wayside Chapel, where I'd been found weeping one morning. In the remaining months of 1987, I worked in a roadhouse, and for a legal firm, and in a fruit shop to earn money to get back to Sydney, to help me make a decision. Would I travel the world, or would I go back to school? Could my friendship with Carita survive our separation? How would I know the best decision to make? How would I avoid being rent with regret?

Before I left Perth, my cousin, who knew all about my John Lennon obsession, gave me *Under the Sun* for Christmas. 'You'll like this,' she said.

I listen to *Under the Sun* as I look out the window of the hot, dry expanses of summertime Australia, stopping for one hot night in Adelaide to ring in the Bicentennial, which I now know not everyone is celebrating. I listen to it on the brown velour couch, after Carita and I try and fail to resume our former closeness. I listen to it as I walk to the Darling Harbour project, saving money to get me back to Perth, to put myself through year twelve, while Carita works to save to travel the world. And it is okay, for that moment, in the Ken Done colours of Sydney, where some celebrate the Bicentennial while others mourn and march, where the harbour glints in the sun and shines with reflected light after the sun goes down.

I listen to 'Dumb Things', nodding my head. Mistakes don't have to be agonised over. Paul Kelly sings cheerfully about the dickhead things he did, and you know he'll probably keep doing the same things next year, and the next, and the next. You can write songs about them, songs that are poetry, songs that are Australian. I've got plenty of dumb things ahead, and for this long dream of a summer, I am ready to welcome them all.

COUNT DOWN THE LITTLE THINGS

LAURA ELVERY

COUNT DOWN THE LITTLE THINGS

Back when such things were still thought possible, Ada's boss, Rose, got an email from a man who called himself Ken – no last name – wanting them to be the first to know he had proof of a live Tasmanian Tiger. Ada was the office girl, and happy for the opportunity. Being office girl at a finance company or a construction company was one thing, but office girl at the Australian Natural History Museum was another thing altogether.

'He's not the first, Ada,' Rose said, unclipping her staff card from her belt and switching it over to a rainbow-striped lanyard.

Rose glanced over at the others in their pod – Colin and Bonnie and Mandy, each at their desk, the smell of burnt toast in the air, and messy stacks of books on the high shelves. Early morning sun flooded in from the single window. Colin was the only one without headphones on and so he swivelled in his chair with his arms on the rests and raised his eyebrows a couple of times.

'Tell me what he said, exactly,' Ada asked them both.

Rose had a PhD. Rose wanted to take Ada seriously. She set her legs apart and folded her arms, nodding. Nobody wanted to be classist about the office girl.

'Yes, all right. What did he say? Well. Says there's a mum, says there's a dad. One baby that he knows of. Apparently just fixed-camera for now. All pretty standard.'

'But you don't believe him.'

'Look, I'd love to,' Rose said.

Colin did the thing with his eyebrows again.

Later, from elsewhere in the building with her office iPad, Rose sent Ada links to a few items. Some of them were part of the museum's own collection, which comprised, as displayed on their rotating website header, *more than 16 million items with more being added every day.* Ada pushed her headphone jack into the flat black box beside her computer and all afternoon she watched the creature pace. The longing, reaching zig of its body. In black and white, its bony skull looked all cavity, all points and ends. Its teeth were hideous and vaguely marine-like. At one point Ada even brought up her hand and touched the computer screen, tracing along the spiny tail.

When she got home, she peeled off her black stockings and put on clean socks. She stood in the kitchen with a mug of soup while she scrolled for more news of Ken and the tiger. Her phone and her laptop dinged with messages from her sister, and her aunty and uncle on their shared account, and a girl she went to high school with, and her ex-boyfriend Jared. *Is it real?* they needed to know. They put all their trust in her, one by one, the replies and questions and jokes overlapping till she almost sent Jared a text meant for her big sister, Cara, with *luv ya x 100* in it.

Hours later, Cara, who was stuck at home with her baby, switched to email. *I want it to be true! Imagine if he's for real. Can't something GOOD just happen?*

Something good.

Sydney, 1890.

Ethel Haywood's first day at university, and she almost hadn't shown up.

Her father had spent years teaching her Latin. Her mother taught her to paint and draw, taught her to sit as still as a stone in the bush, while they waited for creatures to emerge. So it wasn't anything like that – a family who didn't approve. Those were problems for other girls.

Ethel's mother sat hopefully in the kitchen, waiting since the sun rose for her to come down for breakfast. Her father watched her stir the milk into her tea and fiddle with a piece of toast, and Ethel wondered if she could trust herself to make friends, to speak up, to persevere, to not care if she stood out during parties and lectures and field excursions. She hoped, among the other newly permitted young women, that there wouldn't be too much chatter about husbands.

Clearing up from breakfast, neither she nor her parents spoke about school, and their knives on the plates rang very close to her ears. Afterwards, Ethel rushed back through the house to the bathroom. Was this the bit where she vomited quietly? Heaven forbid she felt the need in two hours' time. Last chance to stay. Last chance to go.

In the mirror she soothed herself as though she were a skittish pup. Then she walked straight past her parents, calling out, 'Well, then, goodbye!', not turning back, knowing they'd understand.

The new boots were a silly choice – she'd have to sort those out if she were to walk every day. Her stomach flipped the whole way till she spied the columns and arches, that green lawn, not a window or blade of grass out of place. White galahs dropped to the ground in front of her. The sight of an animal as welcome as the sun.

Move! they seemed to be saying. Keep going!

She answered the birds in her head, All right! Then out loud, 'I'm going!'

Ada messaged Rose to ask for Ken's email. As soon as she pressed send, she agonised over whether such a thing was inappropriate and whether she'd overstepped the mark with the friendly but sharp, blonde-bobbed Rose. Ada had been at ANHM for ten months and she'd recently decided she'd had low-level, non-medicated anxiety for about the same time. Rose thought Ada should go to university. Rose's confidence in her was lovely but also kind of baffling. The federal government had done something to universities six months ago. Bonnie had ranted about it from her swivel chair for a full hour. A tightening of the rules. It was harder than ever for girls like her to go to uni – girls with no money, Ada meant. She knew she was bright.

Two hours later, an email from Rose, no body text, just an *FYI* added to Ken's original subject line, which was: 'urgent: thylacine on winters flat – 28 jan'. In the body of the email Ken had written:

Dear Sir

I used to have a contact at the museum – Prof. Graeme Molloy – who was always thorough in his assessments, but his emails have all come back returned to sender so a helpful young man on your switch gave me this one. Please could somebody give me a call (not email pls I like to speak to a real human).

I've written several books about the thylacine (links below in my email sig) and I can assure you I come with full knowledge and understanding of this magnificent creature. My latest sighting (have had several lately, I suspect all the same family – 1M, 1F, 1 infant) is on Winters Flat, and I'd be happy to drive and collect you since I understand from the helpful young man that your museum's car is no longer in action (damn this shortsighted govt, forgive my French).

I look forward to your call at your earliest convenience.

Ada thought Cara would get a kick out of it, and maybe some hopefulness while she sat at home doomscrolling and breast-feeding, so she forwarded it on, which Rose had never explicitly forbidden. She spent the rest of her day paying invoices, sorting out her timesheets, distributing the minutes of a managers' meeting, and proofreading a brief for the Minister about ongoing risk-management of ANHM programming on the river terrace due to the threat of summer storms. At four o'clock Ada listened to a podcast in which three American economists discussed the effects of Hurricane Gilda on east coast cities. They mentioned, briefly, the California wildfires and – quite touchingly she thought – read out the Latin names of five species of small mammals all suspected now extinct in Alaska.

She texted Cara: *Baby photo, stat!*

Ethel's favourite lecturer set up a meeting with an old friend of his, after class one Friday afternoon at a coffee house in Haymarket. Mr Curthoys was tall, stooped, bow-tied, his face the texture of stony coral. He shook her hand as though she were a man and when he spoke his accent had the urging burr of a Yorkshireman.

'Professor Lumley tells me you're a fine artist. Your interests lie in all sorts of things, big and small.'

'Yes, sir. Wildlife in all its abundance. Last week Professor Lumley invited a conchologist to class.'

'I've never met one of those,' Mr Curthoys said.

'Neither had I. I prefer my creatures a bit livelier than a mollusc.'

'Perhaps with a face?'

Ethel smiled and nodded. The girl brought the tea. Mr Curthoys opened his arms wide in gratitude as though it were a fine banquet being placed before them.

'Miss Haywood, have you ever sold one of your illustrations?' He pointed a dainty finger at the jug of milk and Ethel nodded, watched him pour it.

'Well, my father's bought quite a few.'

'Ha, yes, I hear that a lot.'

Ethel didn't know if it would be better to be the first to speak, or if she should wait. She remembered the pale, probing face of the greyhound she'd seen outside the coffee shop on her way in. The magpie at her window when she woke that morning.

In a rush she said, 'But, Mr Curthoys, if you would like to be the first person beyond the four walls of my house to commission an artwork of mine, I'd certainly accept. Mammals, birds.'

'Shells?'

'Precisely. Whatever you require.'

The only time Ada had ever been to Winters Flat, she'd been fifteen years old – camping with a high school boyfriend and his family. The boyfriend wanted to sleep with her, and she had assumed it would happen here for the first time. It was all rather sweet in the end, at least for the duration of the holiday. His mother was a doctor, or maybe she was a nurse, so Ada asked her to look at a strange mole on her shoulder – although now she marvelled at her own oddness: *What was she thinking?* She'd been intoxicated by the place, having never been anywhere this pretty, never even on the mainland at that stage. Late on the final night camping at Winters Flat, Ada had her first orgasm and for that – and other, more obvious reasons – she would love for Ken to be correct about that mother tiger he said he saw and the father and the cub.

Again she thought about emailing him back herself. Telling him about her love for the grasslands, what she could remember of it. Slightly wooded? Freezing cold? Lots of leaf litter? She could explain who she was and how she – they – were grateful for Ken's exciting email and would be in touch soon. But: enough. Her *verbosity.* This enthusiasm. It was something to keep to herself, to work on, she knew. And she wanted to hold onto her job with Rose.

Ada thought of Rose always rushing off to a different floor of the museum with her iPad under her arm and a tissue tucked into her sleeve. Always swinging that empty aluminium water bottle, forgetting to fill it in time for meetings. Hydration was big in Ada's team; there were posters in the kitchen about it and Mandy was forever getting up to go to the loo.

At five o'clock Ada logged off then took the public lift to level three where a digital projector mounted on the ceiling cast shifting patterns of leaves and vines across the floor – this level was the most theatrical. It was dimly lit with panels in the centre like a nightclub dancefloor. Thin, artful wooden beams were strung from floor to ceiling: the memory of a forest. Ada moved through the silent space. In the far corner, she patted the head – this wasn't allowed – of a run-of-the-mill stuffed pademelon with its fat bottom and pleading toddler eyes. In clear perspex cabinets were a furious-looking wombat, a bedraggled sugar glider and a long-legged dingo on the stalk.

Where would they put Ken's tiger?

He'd posted a video. Which of course had gone viral. Ken and his sweet pink face, his soft bald head and jaunty red handkerchief around his neck, all of it slightly off-centre and breathy as he spoke to the camera in a field.

Downstairs in the central hall was a floating orca, near the gift shop where you could buy an orca pen, packets of orca-shaped lollies, an orca tote bag. Would they put the tiger there, pride of place beneath the whale?

Overhead, the leaves changed. Ada pointed her toe onto the floor to catch the silhouette on her shoe, like she'd seen children do. Seen them try to cup the leaves in their hands.

Ada stopped herself: she was already imagining the creature dead, already imagining it and its family killed then skinned then stuffed again.

Crown Street, 1894, and Ethel left the meeting with a feeling of great excitement. She'd met all the men previously – naturalists, botanical painters, wildlife artists like herself – and knew that the amount of work to be shared across the country was smaller than anybody would believe. To be included, to be a peer among them, well, she could hardly believe it.

Then: enough of that! Not helpful, Ethel!

The book would be a modest success but would reach the right people. Enthusiasts and experts would pore over it, and with any luck make it into the hands of half a dozen members of the

Zoological Society of London. The printing, too, would be high quality and produced right here in Sydney by Dowrick & Sons. So of course she said yes to Mr Curthoys when he presented her with the contract. Ethel murmured a yes under her breath when she signed her name. E.K. Haywood. Well, that could be anybody, couldn't it? E.K. Haywood printed just out of frame beneath the creature's strutting little paws padding across leaf litter.

Now to find it.

Ethel strode to the station. Right before she got on the train she lifted her boot. Bird droppings. Again. Meant to be good luck.

Ada had agreed to babysit Cara's daughter, Isla, for a few hours so she headed there after work, driving the icy streets in her old white Suzuki. Ada's friends all talked vaguely about getting electric cars, but that was years away. It was a ten-minute drive and she stopped on the way at the servo to buy an ice-cream to eat once the baby was in bed. Her last boyfriend, the one before Jared, didn't exactly call her fat but he noted the calories in the food they prepared together in their small flat, and got her to send him a rundown of what she ate during the day to record them at night on a chart on the fridge – his calories too, so for a while it seemed sort of reasonable, like a shared family calendar. She'd been thinking about buying an ice-cream all afternoon at her desk. More invoices, more briefs for the executive team, no word from Rose about Ken's proclamation, even though his selfie-video was all over the internet. More texts from Aunty Elle and Uncle Tony getting excited up in Armidale, another from Jared where he called it a Tasmanian devil instead of tiger, a photo of baby Isla with her face filtered by stars, and a little brown nose and bear ears.

After her bath, the baby pretty much went to sleep right away, which was slightly disappointing. Ada took a book from her bag and the ice-cream from the freezer and lay on the fat white sofa. Half a page in, she placed the book face down on her belly and unlocked her phone. The aftermath of Hurricane Gilda had claimed another twenty-five lives including a whole family, just like that, wiped out. Five or six stories down the page was Ken's video again, this time with a quote from an expert urging caution, plus a raft of audience comments underneath.

Go Tiger Man Go!

We stan TigerKen!!

Um not bloody likely??

Praying and hoping

Honest to god his sweet sweet face

What would it mean for other biodiversity etc etc if this appeared just out of the blue?

Here's a link … they want to bring back the mammoth too!!

Ada went through and liked all the nice Ken ones.

Ethel took the train up into the Blue Mountains. The sky was a rich and welcoming shade, and she took note of it in her journal. Did she have a colour to match? The trees slotted against the blue – tall and powerful gums at the top of the main street – and she stopped to sketch those as well. Ethel's satchel was snug against her hip, and it contained her paper, her boxes of pens and charcoal. Wandering the street towards the walking track up into the hills, she was proud of the satchel and how she might look – surely none of these men outside the bank or the mother with the baby waddling along on the stone fence suspected such an ordinary-looking woman of having anything interesting going on in her mind.

They gathered to celebrate Mandy's birthday with a pavlova Colin had made. At the centre table in their pod, he unlidded containers of kiwi fruit and strawberries, sliced a passionfruit in half. He handed Ada a big spoon and she swirled it through the bowl of whipped cream.

Colin said, 'That Ken guy was on ABC Breakfast.'

'It's a bit sad – all the attention.' Bonnie was new to the museum, recruited back out of retirement, and she liked to proclaim her commitment to the truth, to evidence. She'd been on a panel about the Burrell photos a few years back. 'Poor fella.'

At Colin's nod, Ada dolloped the cream onto the cake. Colin was an artistic man, a devoted curator of cultural objects, especially the collection's rare zoological books from the 1800s. Colin watched Ada and the spoon, nodding as she smoothed carefully.

'He's not the first and he won't be the last,' Rose said.

Mandy said, 'If it all came out true today, this Ken news, then happy birthday to me, I guess!'

'Look, I get it, it's a great story.' Rose took a plate from Colin and spoke with her hands, waving her fork through the air. 'And we love the publicity, right? But should we be doing this to people? Getting their hopes up?'

Rose's mobile rang and the others ate in silence while she talked, everybody else pretending not to listen. Rose said the word Okay very slowly and the word Here?

She hung up. 'Gotta go.'

Ada said, 'Oh, what a shame!' She felt a pang. 'Should we wait?'

Rose looked around at her staff like she was about to say something, but shook her head, glancing down at the phone. She lowered her cake to the table and reached for her iPad and then she was off. Bonnie, Colin and Ada wished Mandy happy birthday again, and they all scraped their plates clean. Rose still wasn't back. Everybody except for Ada had packed up and drifted home.

Alone, Ada texted her sister, asking what the baby was doing and telling Cara to not get her hopes up about the tiger family. Isla had recently started to clap and wave and Ada watched a day-old video three times. Cara finally replied: *Am feeling low about the whole state of the world!! Just here with my exquisite baby contemplating ecological collapse!!* The selfie she sent was of the two of them in the backyard, leafy branches in the background sticking out like antlers from Isla's head. *Our first fawn of the season :))* But Ada could tell Cara's heart wasn't in any of it.

And then Rose was rushing down the hall towards Ada, alone in the office.

'Ada!' she called. Her eyes were bright.

Ethel searched for a day then stayed a night in town above the pub. In her narrow bedroom, she laid out her charcoal and pens on the table. She drew a banksia for fun, from memory, and the face of her childhood cat. She practised her signature.

Before dawn, unable to sleep, she got out of bed and dressed warmly, packing her satchel once more with the lunch from the old lady publican, then shut the door behind her.

The mist rose across the valley, and all was silent except for the sharp call of an eastern whipbird, a pair of Lewin's honeyeaters. On the way up, Ethel delighted in crunching sticks beneath her boots. The city felt impossible from here. The whipbird called again, and a burly creature crashed through the undergrowth, too big to be hers. A yellow-tailed black cockatoo dipped down from a branch and she followed its movement through the air down, down, down the trunk of the tree. Something in its movements told her to keep very still. *Here*, the cockatoo's arrowed body said. Ethel's eyes found the hollow in the tree.

The creature's front paws rested on a low branch and its two hind legs were higher up. It had a poky, plucky look. A ripple sailed across its furred back like a kitten urging a pat. It turned his head.

She would colour it by hand. Somebody from the Zoological Society of London would study her picture at a desk, the book open on a plate by E.K. Haywood. Her own little tiger quoll – drawn and coloured, not shot and stuffed – might even be in a museum one day.

Her *Dasyurus maculatus*.

Across the country there must be thousands of them, possibly millions. But nobody had ever drawn this one.

It fixed its bright eyes on Ethel. They breathed in together.

EVERY FUCKING CITY

ROBBIE ARNOTT

EVERY FUCKING CITY

Around the time I was finishing university, a lot of people I'd studied with were planning trips to Europe. They were going to spend their summers flitting between old cities of old empires. Towards the end of semester, between lectures and at house parties, they discussed their itineraries: Paris, Rome, Barcelona, London, Dublin, Berlin, Prague, Vienna. Perhaps a trip to Portugal. Maybe something sauna-related in Scandinavia. Most of them had been to some or all of these cities before, and spoke with casual authority about the differences between these places, as well as what to prioritise while there. *You have to do this. You must see this. You'd be a fool to miss that.* Young heads nodded sagely at each other. I wanted to scream.

And more than scream: listening to these conversations made me want to break windows, smash letterboxes with a cricket bat. Not because I wasn't as well travelled as these people (I wasn't particularly interested in travel). And not because I was unable to afford a trip such as the ones they were planning (I'd saved a bit of money while working in a bookshop throughout my degree). No – it was because all their holidays sounded the same. Europe this, Europe that. Don't you want to be different, I wanted to ask them? Aren't you sick of doing expected, predictable things?

There's a whole world to go be a tourist in – what's so special about Europe? Why are you all going there? Haven't you heard that Paul Kelly song?

I didn't realise that in my condemnation of their choices I was being as predictable as they were – for every young Australian who has ever gone to Europe, there must surely by a counterpart at home calling them a phony. The condescension of a young person who considers themselves different and deeper than their peers – is there anything more irritating? Is there anything more boring?

I'd also got the song all wrong.

When I'd first heard it, I'd taken 'Every Fucking City' pretty literally. A young man travels around the ancient metropolises of Europe, half-heartedly chasing an on-and-off lover. He leaves each city a little more jaded, a little more bitter, and comes to conclude that these storied places aren't too different from one other. He's failed to be enlightened by travel. He's failed to reunite with his ex. He's failed to find the appeal of these fabled places. Every fucking city is the same.

I've liked the song ever since. At first, it was partly because it reaffirmed my own opinion at the time: that travel doesn't change people, that change can only come from within, and that all my well-travelled peers weren't better or wiser than I was. But it was also because I liked the protagonist – that cool, world-weary, jaded sort of young man who was so similar to the person that I imagined I was (the sort of person I suspect many young would-be writers imagine they are). He wasn't wowed by all those old cities; he was too smart for that.

Of course, I wasn't cool or world-weary or jaded at all. At best,

I was annoying. And of course, the protagonist of the song wasn't immune to Europe's charms; he was just too miserable to notice them. And of course, the song isn't about the cities at all. It's about the protagonist's mistakes, it's about the lover he can't catch (or can't bring himself to catch up to), it's about how love cuts you, how it wrecks you, how it leaves you. It's about how, as the great man sings elsewhere, 'love like a bird flies away'. It's about the numbing of life that follows the departure of love. I wish I'd known that, back then. I wish I'd been able to hear it in his voice.

I did go travelling when I finished university, although not to Europe. I went to Japan. I was going to go by myself, but I'd just fallen in love with a girl, and convinced her to come with me. We both loved Paul Kelly, but she worked in a pub and had grown weary of hearing cover artists play 'To Her Door' every night, so on the trains of Japan we mostly listened to Bob Dylan.

But when we returned, Paul Kelly was back on the menu. And suddenly, I understood 'Every Fucking City'. Maybe it was because I was little older, a little humbler. Maybe it was my experience travelling (how galling!). Maybe it was because I was properly, fully in love, and could now hear the understanding of that feeling in Kelly's wry delivery of the song. Whatever it was, I felt the need to apologise to people – to my girlfriend, to the friends I'd so harshly judged, even to Paul Kelly himself – although of course I never did.

In the years that followed I saw Paul Kelly play four or five times. At musical festivals, at cultural festivals, at his own gigs. Each time I hoped he'd play 'Every Fucking City', but he never did. I became sanguine about the matter. He'd clearly moved on from the song, and I took it as I sign that I should, as well.

Then, in July of 2021, Paul Kelly comes to Hobart with his band. Live music isn't happening in many places, but Tasmania has managed to avoid the worst of the pandemic, so it's still possible, at least in July. The girl I went to Japan with all those years ago and I are now married, and we buy tickets. We line up outside an old theatre, shivering through the Tasmanian winter. Someone in the line mentions that Paul Kelly's first public performance had taken place not far from here, down by the wharves of Salamanca, nearly fifty years earlier.

We file in, get beer, find our seats. The gig is, as expected, terrific. One of the best I've ever seen. It's so good, so transportive, so comprehensive, that I allow myself to hope that this night might be the night it happens. But he doesn't play 'Every Fucking City'.

Afterwards the crowd demands an encore, and he comes back out alone. Here we go, I think. He doesn't need a band to play 'Every Fucking City'. It's going to happen. But he isn't carrying a guitar – it's just him and a microphone. Disappointment grips me, and then I think: maybe he'll sing a stripped back, unaccompanied version of 'Meet Me in the Middle of the Air'. That'd be just as good. But he doesn't. He doesn't sing anything. Instead, he walks to the microphone and begins reciting 'Clancy of the Overflow'.

A few months earlier, my grandfather had died. His favourite book was a collection of Banjo Paterson poems his siblings had given him in 1936 that he'd carried around and read from ever since. The previous Christmas, he'd given it to me. And the night before he died, I'd sat by his bed, reading him 'Clancy of the Overflow'. He tried to grip my arm, but he didn't have enough strength left to curl his fingers, so he just laid them on my wrist. He cried. He said to me: my whole life. I've been reading this poem my whole life.

In that Hobart theatre, hearing Paul Kelly faultlessly recite each line of that poem, this memory swarmed through me. Everything became too hot, too bright, too close. I stopped breathing properly. My wife noticed and reached for me, but I couldn't look at her, because I couldn't take my eyes off Paul Kelly.

This wasn't how this piece was supposed to end. It was supposed to circle back to the beginning, like smart memoir-essays do. It was supposed to twirl back onto my youthful hypocrisy and arrogance, and show how paying close attention to great artists can free you from yourself. But it's not ending like that, because this is what happened, this is what cut me, and the wound is still bleeding, it is still gushing crimson, so this how it ends: Paul Kelly reciting Banjo Paterson in Hobart, a stone's throw from the site of his first-ever gig. He is filling me with my grandfather's death. It's the middle of winter. I am sobbing, my wife is holding my arm, and we are in this same old, cold city that is no longer the same and never will be, because an old man I loved is gone from it, and there is no pursuing him.

BEFORE TOO LONG

JAKE CASHION

BEFORE TOO LONG

BEFORE TOO LONG

For a time beforehand it felt like a stitch, tugging at the body and blurring the world. It could have been an illness, but felt too quiet to cause true harm. Closer to thought than to soul. Closer to object than dream. This meant it couldn't be truly divulged, so he shrugged it off and went about his life.

Then, for one full day, the sky stopped. Clouds held their form. His lover did nothing, as if either bound or catatonic. Static held frozen and children in neighbouring houses and parks stopped growing. Sperm refused tide. Everything was caught.

Then it all started again. The clocks monotonised. The atmosphere wheeled. Laughter broke out from the streets as life returned, unknowing.

But something had left. Something had changed. Because even as the universal pulse commenced again and the clouds were full of alteration like any other day, even as the children unfroze and began again their growth into disintegration, even as the moon once again altered the tides waiting absolute command, he knew he was now sinking. He knew that he was now on the second part of existence, that this day was the palindromic rupture of his life, and from that time onward he was sinking into everything and his reign of time was in reverse. Death was now closer than birth. This was the day of being exactly halfway through.

Not long after, a hole opened in time.

He heard a tear through what had always been impenetrable. It appeared in the kitchen. He approached it, shaking. He looked through the opening and saw many versions of himself in varying stages of younger ages also looking down the hole. It had torn through the past like a giant cylinder. Each self was in the midst of their day-to-day, caught unawares. There were perhaps thirty of them. At the very end of the tunnel, standing with a small stuffed lion in one hand and looking all the way through, past what was, straight to him, was his five-year-old self.

It stared through time with a countenance of placidity and knowing, straight to him as he was now, older and terrified. He turned his head to see if there were older versions of himself, but the tunnel ended here. Behind him was just the small kitchen as it normally was.

The rest of the ages seemed to figure out quite quickly that the small child had no need for them and one by one ceased peering through the hole to resume their lives.

Then it was just the two of them left in the straight and empty passageway. He looked down to the young self, still and bewildered. He felt cold. He looked at the tunnel, expanding and retracting like waves, bringing the staring child right beside him then suddenly pushing him far off like the speck of a tree on a dusked horizon.

Then, as if a tide had decided to settle on shore for unnatural rest, the tunnel closed with a calm and slow sigh, leaving the child standing in the room beside him.

When his lover returned home, putting down bags on the kitchen bench, she found the two of them at the small table, looking up at her with twin sets of eyes. She leaned back on the bench, almost falling. He got up to help her but she put an arm up in protest, stumbling back and closing the door to the living room behind her. He sat back down. The child stared. They continued to sit in silence.

Eventually she opened the door, pushing it slowly as if it were heavy, solid steel behind which was death or comparative evil. She peered from around it, shuddering at the sight. She mustered confidence and closed the door behind her. She sat at the table, looking from one to the other.

'Why's it here?' she asked.

'I don't know.' The child looked at her in rigorous study. She looked back at the child, then turned away. She put her hands to her face. She stood up again suddenly and went upstairs. They both watched her go. When she was gone, they looked back to one another. He sighed. He went to the fridge and got a beer.

He remembered his mother. Their mother.

'Purgatory exists. It's between life and death and we grow its inhabitants and allow them residence in lived and lost years.'

His dying mother had talked in waning lucidity about everything she could seem to grasp with words. She spoke mostly of a tunnel. She said it was there, right there in the room, opening bigger and bigger and swallowing her and her death and all that she had been. She supposed, she gasped in her watery failure, that this was probably what everyone went through but theism had boasted the bigger imagery. There she was, using her dying breaths to talk about her infant self standing far away in a tunnel then suddenly over her like a ghost and taking her away. She used those last breaths to explain the woe of regret instead of one last sentiment to her loving, crying family surrounding her, watching her mind disintegrate before her body did.

If their mother was still with the child, he did not know whether to envy him.

'What is inevitable?' she had asked him near the end, almost with her last words. She had been raised upon God's malice and had swollen ideas of control and free will. This had rubbed off on him.

'What is inevitable?' the child whispered in his ear when he was trying to fall asleep that night.

'I am,' he said. There was no reply, and his lover heaved a sob on the other side of the bed.

Over weeks the child appeared and disappeared, moving up and down on time like a small creature resting on the chest of a sleeping giant, but eventually it was there in the house every day. As its presence grew, his lover grew even more distant than she had been for the years before. Life moved further into its second half and away from the rupture ceaselessly, blending his days, compressing emotions and events and life into a thin line that had to be balanced upon with both banal and exhausting concentration.

She moved in and out of his days like the child moved through time. He watched them both like an unwanted audience, unable to speak to either. When he saw her in passing, she nodded, her eyes down. In bed they hugged and gripped their respective edges as if gravity was liable to rotate during the night and lose them to the cosmos forever.

She had not mentioned the child again. He pictured her displeasure as so prevalent in her that it was almost wearing her as a costume. So when he came home from work one night to find the two of them sitting together, he felt as if he'd uncovered infidelity. She looked up in shock. The child stroked his stuffed lion in his lap with a mug of hot chocolate before him. The three were still, and he immediately felt that he was the intruder.

'Like a mother or a lover?' he asked her. She lowered her eyes, turning back to the child. She sipped her wine. He stormed upstairs to the spare room, loudly and ashamed of his jealousy.

Not long after, the old man appeared.

He felt sick. This was his face as it would be near the end. A callous, sullen face. His eyes were red and they were jaundiced. His teeth were broken, his mouth an abyss nothing good could climb from. The old man did not speak but opened his mouth intermittently to catch up on oxygen in pained increments. A smell rose from it that he recognised had been above his mother's departure.

When his lover saw the old man, she doubled over with incredible flair as if she were on the black stage. She coughed up sickness at the scent of her future lover. She crumpled on the floor. Even when it was gone its smell lingered on the edges of the room. He helped her up and she shook her head, pushing past him to the table. She silently wept, her face in her hands.

'Don't act so sanctimonious,' he said. 'You're out there, too.'

'But I don't hate myself enough to announce it,' she said.

He came downstairs one morning after a troubled sleep. She no longer slept in the bed. When she was home, she was quiet, either behind a glass of wine or a book, floating in rooms that did not contain him, mostly the spare room, which she had made her own. The door was open and it was empty.

That morning the child was sitting at the table, still, in the cold with a quilt around its shoulders.

'Where is she?' he asked.

The child looked around the emptiness between them both. He did the same but did not know why. Their eyes met again. He turned away, putting the kettle on and leaning his face over the steam. He made hot chocolate for the child and coffee for himself. He sat down opposite.

'You don't act like a five year old.'

'Neither did you.' They drank. Outside the garbage truck growled in diesel and hydraulic with the first noise from the cold morning.

'I love her,' the child said.

'Like a mother or a lover?' A smell wafted over the room. They turned to see the old man in the corner. It looked more decrepit than it had when it had arrived. He shuddered.

'Do you look at me the way I look at him?' he asked the child.

'How could I possibly know that?'

She did not return his calls. Her mother would not say with direct words if she was there or not. Her office, too, followed a given script of ambiguity. Soon he accepted her absence as an almost. Most of her things were still there, that the rent was never unpaid, but she was gone, and that was that.

He went about his days with practised monotony. The child was more present than ever, and morose with her gone. The old man, too, was appearing more often. Its smell was almost always in each room he walked through, and no matter how much he aired out the house it sat atop the scents he'd lived with before the second half of life, and as months wore on, continued to flourish in pungency. The child made a point of being around during his most trivial moments. The nights that had once been allocated for shared dinners of high, then continuously waning, sentiment for the couple had been replaced with solitary drinking in which he was free to listen to the old songs that unlocked shadowy, mystical orbs of retrospect blurred enough so that he was a minor king in old, precious situations. He'd drink and smile and sing and then the child would appear and ruin his catharsis and nostalgia.

Sometimes the old man watched, too.

One night he and the old man sat side by side. He had taken to scolding it and simply pretending the child didn't exist.

'Did you have a grotesque caricature invade your house, too?' he asked the old man. It did not answer. He shook his head and drank. He thought about attacking it. He thought about hugging it. He did nothing. He was terrified of it.

The old man walked around, slowly and painfully, half there and half not, looking at aspects of the house like a bored pet. He stood in the corner of the room, staring into sharp blankness and dispelling scent as if marking a non-existent territory. He could see in the corner of his eye a dark spot seeping into the walls, and he shook his head and drank.

'If you're where I'm headed,' he said, 'what more is there to be afraid of?'

Nothing replied and months began to float over him with urgency.

He was drinking on the couch, on a rare evening of being unbothered by the two, when she walked through the door. He spilled his drink in uncontrolled movements undirected at anything and trying to be everything and she put a hand up to calm his excitement, gently closing the door behind her. He'd imagined his chiselled demeanour she would return to if she ever came back, but all coolness and control disappeared into the shag.

'Is he here?' she asked. He stopped. He stayed poised uncomfortably, half on the couch and half in the wet patch of his unawares. She walked past, going through to the kitchen and closing it behind her. After a while he came to and followed.

She was sitting at the table with the child on her lap, stroking the head that was tucked in her breast. Her eyes were closed and the child looked almost asleep. He leaned on the counter and stared.

'Then you came back for me, too,' he said. She shook her head in a slow, peaceful rhythm. The child breathed deeply and calmly in her arms, the lion pushed up to his cheek.

'This is perverse,' he said at last. Again she shook her head.

'I finally found you,' she said.

'It's a child.' She shook her head yet again as if in a fugue. With the child still in her arms, she gently stood. She looked over at him once, a blank, noncommittal look, before going to the stairs and retiring. He was left with a wet sock, staring into a noncommittal nothingness between the stairs and a smoky apparition of the old man gradually appearing like condensation nearby.

Over the next few weeks the small house became two halves whose boundaries contorted with the movements of its occupants, cutting through levels and rooms, keeping the stench and him within one, and her and the child within the other. He heard her muttering and laughing through the walls. He heard within her muffled voice a depth and a love he thought was a false memory. The days kept on moving, days that had already happened to him happening again as he slowly moved through the second half of life, just as banal as when he had lived them before and occurring again in cruel jest. He realised that the only progression of life was decay and how one dealt with such. He acted accordingly.

He sat at the table with a drink, eyes unfocused on the first page of a simple book. He raised them to the old man sitting in silence on the other side. Upstairs he heard laughter. He put the book down, looking at the face before him. He stared hard at the sunspots and cancers, at where his hair was already beginning its retreat and where it would eventually fall back to. He looked at the puffed and unclear eyes, the cataracts blowing holes in the universe he supposed was outside the old timer, himself included.

Unsure and inevitable.

He sipped his drink and thought about the liver with its masses. He thought about the wearied brain, the neural halls expanding in fog and blackness where the little lights of knowledge found it harder and harder to navigate. Somewhere in there was he, walking in darkness.

Upstairs laughter exploded again. He threw his drink at the wall, finding brick behind paint and it smashed into flashes of wet and amber. He stormed upstairs, opening the door to the spare bedroom. They were splayed on the rug, their happiness put on temporary hold at his presence.

'You can take him,' he said. 'I don't care about it. Have him. Just leave.'

'That's all we've wanted,' she said. The child said nothing.

'Then you have my blessing. If that's what you were waiting for. Take him.' He hesitated at the door and walked back downstairs. He made another drink then cleaned the floor where the remains of wet glass had fallen. The old man watched him from his chair.

He drank quickly. Then he had another. He went back to staring at the old man, keeping his eyes fixed in study as he raised the glass to his lips. The old man's face did not change. It breathed with pain, it watched with apathy.

'If I fear you,' he said to the old man, 'then life is already complete.' He drank again. The old man continued its silence.

'Did you feel the rupture, too?'

It did nothing to indicate hearing him. Perhaps it was deaf. Perhaps he would go deaf.

'Do you remember a day when everything reversed?'

From above he heard the opening and closing of drawers and the zipping of bags. Their preparations went on and on and eventually the noises faded from his senses. He became present. He could not stop staring at the imperfections of age. They were chilling, and belonged to him.

They belonged to him.

What is inevitable?

I am.

He thought about the three of them. Disjointed but in the same place. He thought of his life's true judge and he found it sitting before him, wheezing and dishevelled, his greatest foe, fear and accomplishment.

'So there's nothing left to be afraid of.'

Then he nodded. Then he smiled. His first in months. He even laughed a little, taking another swig.

'If you're my fate.' The old man didn't reply, instead getting up out of his chair with a sound like an old bag of breaking sticks being thrown over a shoulder, and slowly he walked out of the room. He watched him go, still smiling, still nodding, not even sure if it understood him.

'I love you, old man.'

They came downstairs. She held his hand and a bag in the other, descending in feeble balance. She saw him in a state of quiet jubilation, laughing and muttering to himself. She put the bag down heavily.

'What's gotten into you?'

He looked at her. His lover. He stood, then walked over to them. He kissed her on the cheek. A sharp, platonic touch that seemed to sting. Then he touched the child's hair before she pulled him away from his reach. He nodded to them both, then sat back down.

'He will grow up,' he said, pointing to the child without looking, 'and he will live in the mediocre and dream in the grandeur. Love what is, my dear. This only happens once and so it happens infinitely.'

'You've lost it,' she said. She hurried the child out in front of her through the kitchen behind him. He heard her say something to the child. Then she came back into the room, grabbing her bag. He turned to her and spoke.

'Before too long it will be the time of our demise and the

creatures that grow from it,' he said with an excited slur. 'Where you see a monster, I have fallen in love. You have fallen in love with possibility. That is the terrifying chance you take. So go with it. Take it bundled. It is not mine any longer. I see what fate determines. If I were to live this day, this life, a million times over, it would still be that old man who stands before me, and I would embrace his presence a million times over.' She shook her head in disgust. She went to say something, but stopped short, and without speaking walked back out of the room.

'I feel peaceful now,' he said to her back. 'Maybe for the first time since I was his age. Tell him that.' She didn't turn, nor indicate she had heard him. The front door opened then closed again in finality.

'I feel peaceful now.' He took another drink.

A stench seemed to be growing around him, emanating from his body. The old man emerged before him, looking to the door its life had just walked out on and would so again for eternity, but he was in the corner smiling to himself, alone and lost in false bliss, and could see neither warning nor despair.

SOFT BITE

ALICE BISHOP

SOFT BITE

Just take care of it, okay? Minna says, the day's eyeshadow worn off but still gathered, thick and shimmering, in the creases of her lids. The house feels smaller than usual, its mudbrick walls dusty and caramel. A yellow sponge, still soaked, sits darkened and heavy by the kitchen sink.

How? Dean asks, wide hands hanging.

For once, just work it out, Minna continues. *I can't do everything,* she pauses, almost pleading, *everything and also this.*

Dinner would normally be on, maybe a supermarket chook with coleslaw or pasta with lemon cream. Something simple, anyway, served with two tins of beer. Yana – her nappy printed with cartoon ponies, pale hair wild – would be watching for wallabies through the back window, dusk dropping lilac across the ridge. The patient dog would normally be waiting under the kitchen table for dropped scraps.

Good boy, Dean might've said, slipping the heeler – his fur dappled and mangy – an edge of buttered bread.

Yana baby, Minna would usually say. *Come back and eat a little bit more please.*

Not now, Yana would answer, her new favourite words.

A softened, recently learned, two-year-old version of no.

Yana, Minna would then say firmly. *Yes, honey. Yes, a little bit.*

It's different tonight. An iceberg lettuce sweats into a bag on the bench. Yana is already somewhere between sleep and awake. Her small, medicated body slack in Minna's arms, who's wrapped her in the woollen blanket usually spread across the bed. The pale blue of her closed eyelids shows through. The dog, usually close, isn't around.

Dean, Minna says, catching her husband staring at their daughter's fresh stitches, poking up like synthetic insect legs from her cheek. He thinks of jumping jacks, ants, that rust-black rush out of freshly dug ground. The sting. *Dean*, Minna repeats, looking at him blankly standing there. *Dean*, Minna announces, louder this time.

Minna, what? Dean says, distracted and not meaning for it to come across as short as it does.

She has everything ahead of her, Minna says. *And now, this …*

Now what, says Dean, sounding more defensive than he intended. He catches himself then pivots – as valley men often do – quickly into defence. *G'on, Minna, go ahead, make a shit situation worse.*

Minna steps towards her husband, something she used to do, years ago, an instinct before after-school fights on dusty suburban ovals – Bacardi blooming through. She pulls her shoulders back to make her small body broader, Yana still drowsy in her arms. *She'll always have a reminder of our shitty parenting now … A fucking scar, Dean, across her face.*

Dirt roads darken along the ridge. Currawongs settle. Minna and Dean stand apart in the crackling lounge room, thinking things they'll never say. The last of the unculled foxes start to leave their dens for a night of searching – for forgotten chooks, sugar glider kits, shaky from first flights, and roadside rabbits, recently hit. Lonely barks, then eerie territorial screams, will later echo along the ridge.

Well, fuck, Dean says, looking down at the puncture wounds across the pad of his left hand, pink holes already puffy from just hours of everyday grit.

You'll have to soak that – salt, Minna says.

Minna, he says. *Min baby*, he says, pleading also a little now. *Sorry. I didn't know he had it in him. No one did.*

Dean had first thought it was something electrical going wrong. A fire-pump generator howl. Yawning, Minna's scream had been like a Commodore burnout breaking the quiet of a sleepy suburban street, a freeway powerline hit. It was a black cockatoo, screeching across the valley – a simple announcement of all that's wrong with the world. Everything unsaid.

Min! Min, I'm coming, called Dean, running in from the woodshed towards the unfamiliar sound. He'd been watching old motorbike clips on YouTube and chopping kindling. A handful of salt and vinegar chips and a plastic lighter lay by the garage sink. *Min!* he'd yelled, again, but then there was just Minna screaming, salt and spit – *Get off, get off, get off.*

Picture books – pastel-coloured covers bent – lay scattered across the floor. A cup of tea had been spilt across the kitchen bench;

Minna's favourite gold-glazed mug lay in pieces. Blood specks patterned the dirty carpet; faces bleed the most, emergency doctors have so often, straightforwardly, said. Yana, uncharacteristically quiet, had just looked up. Bone exposed. All kinds of pink.

Yana, honey, Dean'd said, reaching down to lift her. *Yana,* he said, as the girl started only then to cry, her tiny nails digging through the Dean's faded windcheater and into skin. There was the distinctive smell of fear. That chemical tang, something unfamiliar and metallic. Animal piss. *Yana, honey, baby,* Dean said, again and again. *You're okay, it's okay.*

Minna was kicking like Dean had never seen anyone kick. The sound from her mouth had stopped but it was still moving, opening and closing like she had been underwater for hours and was just, only then, coming up for air.

Minna, hon. Minna, Dean had said, reaching over but staying safely away. *It's okay, please, baby, stop.*

But the blows of Minna's right, scratched-up Blundstone went on – thudding muscle, breaking rib.

Blue Heeler Pups, free to good home, the service station notice board had read. The whole way out to Steels Creek, Minna reached over to Dean from the passenger seat. Her thumb moved in gentle circles under the shaved stubble at the base of his neck.

Yana wasn't around yet; she wasn't born – just ten weeks' worth of gathering cells. Tooth buds forming under pink beginnings of gums.

The vineyards of the valley were clipped back. Horses in padded blankets stood under scraggy sugar gum. Dean joked about wanting potato cakes for lunch, really wanting potato cakes for lunch. Minna thought about hot chips.

We're about to get our baby, Minna said, smiling before briefly checking her mascara in the rearview. *That puppy smell. Needle teeth*, she said. Her excitement made Dean love her even more, sitting in the car with him in her favourite flannel shirt and paint-flecked trackies.

Okay, calm down, Min, he said.

A baby before our baby, she said.

Dean had put his wide hand on her leg, his index ring finger proud under the still-novel gold-band glint.

A grey-haired woman had continued to work on the farm as Minna and Dean arrived. She hadn't paused to offer niceties as most valley women are taught. She hadn't even looked up as Minna and Dean drove their noisy twin cab up the long gravel driveway, lined with thirsty European-style trees.

Got to keep on top of the place, hey, the blue-eyed man welcoming them said, nodding towards the woman across the paddock. *A farm's a lotta work mate*, he said.

Dean nodded in agreement, hands in his pockets. Minna kept quiet.

There had been a moment of guilt about lifting the puppy up from its familiar warmth; there usually is. Dean distracted himself by small talk with the man about his failing alpaca farm. *People don't want to pay for quality, anymore*, the man, hands worn, had said. *The hunger's for cheap stuff online, synthetic shit.*

Guilty of that, mate, Dean said, tugging at this seam of his nylon shirt.

Minna stayed quiet, imagining the life they'd give the puppy, its tiny triangle ears like lamb's tongue weed to touch. The mother's stumpy tail wagged gently as her owner reached down into the blue-roan fur of her last two young left. She whimpered. Then wagged again.

Heeler. But a streak of staffy in him too, mate, the farmer said – announcing this to Dean and not looking at Minna at all.

Righto, Dean said.

Makes them loyal, I reckon.

As the others made small talk above the heeler pups, the working woman continued wielding a brushcutter over the front paddock in long, low sweeps. Special black ankle guards cuffed her socks – stopping burrs and seeds clinging on.

After lowering the chosen puppy into a cardboard box, Dean shook the man's hand. A cloud of white cockatoos screeched something's arrival down by the long paddock dam. Looking back out over the yard, the couple watched as the woman brushcutting stepped back from her work to lean on a fence post. Cigarette smoke floated up from her cap-shadowed face.

Let's call him Mack, Dean had said, Minna in the passenger seat smiling – the tiny dog in her lap.

Mack like the truck or Mack like an old tradie who only eats petrol station sausage rolls?

Like the truck, Dean said, smiling, feeling like a man in control of his life. *Mack like the truck.*

Ok let's, Minna said, the handful of blue-grey puppy softly chewing her thumb. Summer sun warmed the tops of her bare thighs and the sheepskin-furred dash.

It's dark now. The pockmarked moon is full, gently lighting up the hills. Somewhere above a roof-bound ringtail shuffles, maybe a rat, whichever grey-furred animal it is slowly folding from poisoned cubes. Dean had read about how the galahs up north are dying from the stuff, muffled pink-feathered bodies strewn across suburban front yards. It hadn't stopped him lacing the roof cavity with poison; tiny floral op shop dishes heavy with death.

Possum's okay living up there, just leave it be, Minna had said the winter before, Yana sucking blueberry yoghurt from a plastic sack on her lap. *We live out here to be with nature,* she added. *We choose to live here,* she again said, *alongside them.*

No babe, Dean had said. *We can't have that.*

Somewhere on the other side of thick mudbrick wall Minna now lies on the floor with Yana beside the cot. She holds her daughter firm, the small sleeping body warm against a still-whirring chest. Yana's hair smells like disinfectant and a little like coconut shampoo. Minna imagines the silvery scar already forming across her daughter's cheek. She imagines her daughter grown – broad-shouldered and tall – looking back in the mirror at the mark on her face.

You're a beauty, she says, nuzzling into the familiar warmth of Yana's neck.

Yana's cheek was sewn back together with silver tools, saline and sutures. Three hours of nylon and silk. Appointments with follow-up doctors were recommended under fluorescent lights while Dean drank black coffee from plastic cups. Minna watched.

How did this happen again? The hospital social worker asked, softly, assuming all couples presenting at emergency lead with something other than the truth. They were all city people in the white support room. Crisp cologne. Lowered voices. RM Williams boots. *Soft cunts*, a younger Dean maybe once would have said. *No idea about living*, a younger Minna would have agreed. The television in the waiting room adjacent continued playing a documentary about Greece.

I just looked away for a second, Minna answered. *A second, then I heard Yana scream.*

That must have been really frightening, the social worker continued, her feathered eyebrows folding together in a show of empathy. *Were you familiar with the dog?*

It was a neighbour's dog, Dean interrupted. *We were always worried about it: half pitty – pitbull, I mean – a real dangerous thing.*

Half pitty, Minna agreed, feeling the lie crackle in her chest. She toyed with a bit of inner cheek with her tongue, cut loose by her own teeth. She thought about the kicking – only hours before – the spit. Then Dean putting Yana, still bleeding, down to intervene. *Min baby, it's okay*, he'd pleaded, grabbing the dog by the scruff. Wide eyed and panting, the animal had swung around and latched onto his left hand. *Fuck!* Dean had said, starting, then, to kick too. The dog, whimpering, quickly let go of its grip.

You need to lodge it with the police, said a different young nurse – small diamond flowers pinned the length of her left ear. Dean thought she looked no more than twenty. She reminded Minna of herself, years ago, before she even thought of things like having a husband or a kid. *Then local laws*, the flowered girl continued.

Yes, thanks. We will, Dean said.

It's very important you do, sir, she said.

What kind of parents even are we? Back from the hospital, pink crumpled prescriptions cover the coffee table. Yana's blood – maybe the dog's – already russet and hardened, speckles the floor. Minna looks at Dean across the room, Yana now sleeping.

Minna, Dean's left hand has already started to throb, bits of everyday grit settling into puncture wounds. *Tell me what to do and I'll do it, babe,* he says, whispering now. Another plead.

Take care of it; I need to get her to bed, Minna answers.

What do you want me to do? Dean asks again, his voice trailing after Minna walking down the hall, lined with pictures of Yana from before. Something in the roof shuffles, scratches, then stills. Outside a feral cat has caught a common dunnart, its small grey-furred body limp between teeth.

The dog sits by the fire, panting pink the way injured things do.

Stay, be a good boy, Dean used to be able to say – leaving his jacket outside any pub or shop. And the heeler would wait there. Hours. All kinds of people knew the dog, leaning down to pat its dappled head. *Hi Mack,* older women in lilac woollens would say. *Hey, matey,* tradies, stopping for valley coffee before hours of dirt works, would pass and say. But the dog wouldn't even look up, its eyes on the door.

The lights from the garage shine a soft light, a gold light, along the edge of the house – flecks of insect rushing to warmth. No streetlights mean there are stars.

A good dog, Dean says, grabbing Mack by the scruff and dragging the animal out to the shed. *You've been a good boy.*

The dog, loyal but unsure, whimpers. It whines.

The tartan picnic blanket comes from the back of the Hilux. The shovel is one of three from the yard. The rope, although Dean isn't yet sure how he'll use it, comes from the cupboard above the garage sink.

Dean takes his windcheater off, laying it on the cold concrete ground.

What the fuck have you done? Minna asks, her hand reaching towards the rug on the floor. It's late now, eleven pm. Dean only knows this because the loungeroom fire has burned down to just a glow. It's quiet, except for the footy replays he has put on to drown out the white noise.

Please don't tell me that's the dog, Minna says, and for a moment Dean hears the dog scrambling again – its short nails scratching, desperately, against the chalk-rainbowed garage floor.

Minna, Dean says, like her name will calm her down.

Tell me you took him to the vet?

I took care of it.

You didn't kill him yourself, Minna says, *tell me you didn't do it yourself*… It's then she holds her small hand to her woollen chest, her eyebrows – thick and dark – fold down. Dean notices a hole in the fabric of her left knee. He looks over to see what she sees, a rug-covered lump, a rope pull-toy and the tip of a lilac tail poking through.

What have you done? Minna says again.

Minna, Dean says. *You told me to. It's done.*

LOOK SO FINE
FEEL SO LOW

KIRSTEN KRAUTH

LOOK SO FINE FEEL SO LOW

LOOK SO FINE FEEL SO LOW

I've been seen on the street

My street doesn't change much during lockdown. It's always quiet. The beautiful trees lose their leaves, grow them again. But the magpies and parrots seem louder and more bold. The crows beat their sticks on the electricity poles. The cockies eat all the pears. Every year I say I'll get a net. I sit on the front verandah each morning with a coffee, no matter the weather. It keeps me connected to the world. The man who gardens across the street every day, the soft percussive sound of his rake. He has six green bins that go out on Sunday nights. The woman two doors down who leaves a basket of lemons perched precariously on her letterbox for anyone to pick. My kids head up to the café for a two-litre milk that will be gone by the end of the day. A man rides by on a penny farthing. I'm serious. It is Castlemaine, after all.

Wearing brand new clothes

I always fall for a man in a suit. The first time I see the muso on stage, just before the fires, just before the pandemic, he has sharp creases and wears black. I check him out later on YouTube. He's decked out. Waistcoats. I can't imagine him in shorts. More Brunswick than Bondi. Coming back from a dalliance with him interstate, I see a guy at the airport with a Total Tools singlet on. I'm affronted and text him. I know it will make him laugh. When my novel is released into the early wilds of COVID, I wonder what I'm going to wear at my self-styled Zoom event. I go full eighties: *Flashdance* t-shirt, leopard-skin skirt, metallic pink leggings. Being in my own space inspires me to be dazzling. I rope in my kids to do a reading. I think about dancing up the empty streets with my ghetto blaster pumping out the mixtape soundtrack to my novel. A party for one. But the mood of the empty streets is not one of celebration.

I guess I've landed on my feet

With all my festivals cancelled, I have Bellingen marked on the calendar for eighteen months. I wait. Leading up, there's a lunar eclipse. I watch it with my kids and friend Jason who comes to visit for a week from Sydney. The kids crowd around him excited at the idea of another person actually allowed in the house and we eat haloumi pizza and play movie trivia. The next morning, the Victorian government decides on a snap lockdown. I can't bear to miss out on my one event. It's two weeks away. I start packing the car. The kids are already at school. I kiss Jason and apologise. I drive off not knowing where I'm going. I get across the NSW border with an hour to spare. By night-time I'm winding my way across the Snowy Mountains heading to Tathra. Google has led me here. It's starting to rain. Signs say I should have snow chains. I think about stopping the car and sleeping in my clothes with the engine and heater running. Shadows lure me in the dark. I turn at a sign that has a caravan on it. Jason texts me to say that after I left, there was an earthquake that shook all the windows. I'm in a cabin on a freezing night and my body keeps up the journey going around the bends. When I wake up, I'm on Miles Franklin Drive in Talbingo, next to a beautiful lake; not the precipitous mountainside I imagined in the dark. In the next fortnight my car breaks down and there's a sudden snowstorm and I have to fly to Bellingen from Merimbula. I wonder if the universe is trying to tell me something.

I'm a lucky guy I suppose

I'm watching the camellias blossom out the bathroom window. Again. Last year at this time it was the same. I go out to the huge camellia tree and I pick the flowers and drop them into a bucket. I run a bath and I pour them in. Rich hues of pinks and reds, wet folds, oily in the water. I lie down under them and they are soft on my body. My toes peek out. The petals curl and the green leaves go glossy. They have names like Cherry Glow, Dream Lover, Early Pearly. Soft light moulds my body in an angel shape. The pure glint of sun frames a tub. A Cleopatra in the milky spring that's budding as it always does.

She tells me that she loves me

I remember the first time I experience real charisma. Sam Worthington, the actor, walks into a room where I'm working, an industry function. And it isn't just a this-guy-is-hot but a raw-flesh presence that the whole place feels, one that seems to occur in spite of him, a gravitational pull, yes, this magnetic drawing-to and I wonder about this exchange of energy. Does this charisma come from a power dynamic where I have watched and listened and taken him in, but the reverse is not true? Can it wear off? The first time I meet the muso in the flesh I sniff him out. Pure animal. In the elevator I rub his arm and say, 'So you're really real then?' He is so attentive at first. He pours his heart out into songs for me. We share a rich world of longing and language-play and I listen to his music and see the possibilities. And the similarities. So many similarities. He is excited about my writing and he encourages me to work on new projects and collaborate. But a few months in, after my book launches, the tone starts to shift. He tells me I shouldn't celebrate my book on social media the way I do. That it's not fair on other writers like him.

She buys me things

My kiddo looks online for clothes to order. There is a non-binary flag in purple, yellow, white and black. They get a hoodie and t-shirt. Slogans that help things make sense to me. Like everything – on the spectrum. Somewhere in between. 'Are you a boy or a girl? No.' We laugh at that. They ask me where I fit. I say, 'I'm more and more keen on non-binary because of your influence.' I'm realising how much gender comes into it. All day long. I struggle with the pronouns. I want to do the right thing. They ask, 'Do you have crushes on boys or girls?' I say, 'I have always had crushes on both. Gender never really comes into it for me. I feel a very strong attraction to the person, regardless. It doesn't happen very often but when it does, bam!' They ask if they can buy a t-shirt that says they are bisexual. I baulk. 'You can't walk around saying you're bisexual when you haven't even had a sexual experience yet.' When the non-binary-coloured hoodie arrives, they wear it every day for the whole school holidays. We go to the movies and they blob a big bit of chocolate stain down the front that remains to this day. They are so proud of standing out, of shining in their identity.

She wants to take care of me

He shares a few tales of trauma and depression and I worry over him. I send him links to my favourite books to read in tough times like *When Things Fall Apart*. But I push away little things that might grow into big things. The fact that he could have a girlfriend overseas. The fact that he won't give me his address. The fact that he never advertises his gigs until the day before. The fact that he doesn't seem to have any online presence. The fact that he wants to exchange messages and fantasies in private conversations and an encrypted app where our words explode, untraceable. The fact that he gets angry every time I try to call him on the phone to chat in person. The fact that his friends of thirty years don't know the same stories I do. The fact that his anger and pain rains down on me in sharp words that bury under my skin like acupuncture needles.

And all I gotta do is sing sing sing sing

I write my first song after our first dalliance. It is not a love song. It is full of menace as if it is the opening lines of a crime fiction novel.

It's about fire and glass breaking and a well-worn pattern into a forest and being locked in a sweet cage. The first time we meet, the streets in Sydney are empty because of the smoke and we watch the bats fly across the dusk sky in Chippendale. The fires. The bats. In lockdown I send my budding lyrics to a best friend. The next morning he sends me songs, voice rough on the phone. I lie in bed listening to these precious gifts. How different from writing a novel. Or even poetry. To receive your words back as music. I write a song a week. By the end of the year I have an album of songs. I start to sing. Writers talk about trying to find their voice. I look for mine, full-throated, a means of embodied expression, inescapable. I sing out the sadness. And the memories now surfacing that I don't want. I notice that musicians don't talk publicly about who inspires their songs. The lyrics go places a novel can never go with their immediate emotional resonance. There are so many ways to do the instrumentation. I want melancholy with a beat. I pick up a guitar and like millions of others around the planet I start to learn.

Well I look so fine but I feel so low

There's a video of him sitting by the water with his guitar. He's sorry to all of us, he says. He screwed up this time. Again. The week before I head off to Bellingen, I make a report and hand it to the police. The rage and manipulation. The quiet menace where he approaches my friends and family online. I learn the meaning of terms. Coercive control. Emotional abuse. Gaslighting. I put on my investigative hat. My journalistic curiosity seems a way to cope with the unfathomable. I talk to the other women in his life. I build a picture of decades-old hurt. A tortured artist. A charmer.

A narcissist. I read *fake*. I worry for all the silenced women. I know they are out there. The ones who aren't so strong and confident in their creative life, in their standing in the community, as me. He's told me about these women. Stalkers. Sick. Delusional. His words, unfounded, but I believed them at the time. He's convincing. I worry for all the future women. That's why I write this.

She takes me by the arm

When I get back from Bellingen, my daughter asks me to lie in her bed. I've been away three weeks. She always tackles me with the curly questions before sleep. It makes me realise how many questions I don't know the answers to. Why won't you get back together with Dad? What's a French kiss and can you give me one? Why won't you have another baby because I want a little sister? This time, it's not a question. 'Mum, I'm non-binary. I don't feel like a girl and I don't feel like a boy.'

She takes me all around

The night before my first Bellingen event, I get vertigo again. I lie back on the strange bed with my head at the wrong angle and the room spins, my eyes caught in a Gravitron loop. The professional photos from the weekend look like I'm glowing. A friend says it's because I've reached the 'dizzying heights'. My body shakes so hard on stage I hold a paper clip in my fingers as if it will help me keep upright. I stand and read with a musician and I keep going to catch the microphone before I realise it is me that's off balance. The audience rolls in front of me like they are on a drunken boat and

I give up on engaging with them. I can't keep myself up. The music stand holds the words and I read them and hope no one can notice my sheeny skin, trembling jaw, rush to get through. Later I wonder why I didn't say it at the beginning. I have vertigo. Please catch me if I fall.

She knows all her friends are talking

My friend tells me what to do when he puffs up like a predator. It is so fun to be pursued at the beginning, I admit it. To be pounced on and ravaged and desire/d. He's in his mid-fifties, I'm in my forties. We're both out of relationships that lasted eighteen years. I never thought this would happen again. All I want is a good standing-up pash, like that one between The Hot Priest and Fleabag. I get it. We feast on each other. In a long-distance relationship, with the isolation of COVID, there is so much erotic space to fall into. We're both writers. Words have extra weight. His early come-on lines? 'You read between the lines. You read me like a book.' My response is, 'When you start reading me, we'll be getting somewhere.' He says, 'I think I am reading you.' And he is right. It starts off exciting and adventurous – all the things I reveal too soon that I want. But down the track it's not so fun to feel hunted when things turn dark, to be trapped in an alley. To feel groomed and played with. It takes months to fully realise it. My friend tells me to look him levelly in the eye. A stance where I will not back down, will not capitulate, but also will not step forward for a fight, to retaliate. I stand my ground.

Saying look what our good girl's found

When I get back, she leans into me. She's ten years old and she tells me what all the letters mean. The LGBTQIA and more. She's done a lot of research into this. 'Are you pansexual?' she asks. I don't know but I do know I'm out of my depth. I say, 'Does this mean you feel like you are a boy and a girl?' She says, 'No, I don't feel like either.' She says, 'I want to be known by they and them.' I think of the plurals and the editing involved. She says, 'I don't like going to the toilets at school now and the one I want to use, which is unisex, is always locked.' I struggle along with all this new information. I don't know where to begin. I hold her hand and feel her strength guiding me and flick between joy and a sense of loss of something intangible. She says, 'If I'm not your daughter, what am I?'

One thing she's got on you

The first thing I see when I turn on Facebook is an ad for his tour. The algorithms are brutal. Unlike me, he can cross borders now. He's heading to Brisbane, Melbourne, Sydney. In the olden days you'd walk out and that was it. You'd have a week of bawling and drinking wine with friends and eating too much sweet and fried stuff and then emotions would slowly dwindle away because you'd never have to see them again. You'd have space to let go. Now there are unwanted hints and reminders. Digital traces. Hashtags. I block him everywhere. The police call to tell him to stay away from me and my friends and family. He doesn't listen. He emails my friend a threat that he's going to take me to court to look into custody of my children. He's never even met them. I send screenshots of these threats to my friends who are lawyers. They hold a mirror up to him. They cut through the nonsense of it. They make me laugh. They talk about risk and behaviour. They ask me what's the worst that could happen. They tell me I can handle it.

She's so easy to impress

I contact him to get a copy of his book. I'm interested in the cross-pollination between music and writing. I like the art that comes from the collision of genres, from making things that don't fit neatly. He contacts me to start the chase. He takes me down the rabbit hole. He wants to eat me and drink me. I read the book in a fire-haze of desire and Tennessee Williams, as the places he talks about in his novel burn in my imagination and then in reality down the east coast. I've watched him and listened to his music for decades. He gets to go past go where others wouldn't. I remember reading an article once on people who are scammed for love. I thought, how could you ever fall for that online? Give up so much of yourself? He says, 'It turns me on so much that you trust me in this space.'

When she asks me dumb questions

I've done all the dumb things. All the things I tell my kids not to do. There is such a huge gap between the person I know and the person they see. His public persona connects me to times and places and books and music that I've loved: enough that I tell him secrets; enough that I share images; enough that I don't set the boundaries around my heart and my inner world. I see his reputation – a sensitive and talented soul – as something that elevates him, as a security blanket wrapped around me. On the first night we chat online I ask him to send a photo, right now. I want to see his face, that it's him sneaking into my bedroom. Proof. The photo looks different from the person I imagine. The blanket turns out to be threadbare and offers no warmth or comfort. I head out into the cold and force myself to ask the questions I don't want to hear the answers to. A loved one tells me about the hotel rooms in far-off places with others. The women ordered neatly in folders. The undying love-confessions and the photos of body parts. The endless deception. I imagine myself filed and defiled. She tells me that when she finally kicked him out she threw his piano down the stairs. I hear the cascading notes and the symphonic crash and the broken black keys. Pete Townshend and Kurt Cobain can smash their guitars on stage but that's nothing compared to this. The final push and its release. I feel that surge, that rush – the strength of her convictions. 'Don't worry. We're thriving now,' she says.

All I gotta do is say yes yes yes yes

I'm sitting in my bedroom looking out at the blossoms and the empty street. I have never been drawn to the confessional or its idea of catharsis. But my conversations during COVID have started to change the way I write and relate. Friends and strangers reveal things to me; intimate, sad, life-changing, hidden. There are so many stories like mine. The spirit of Grace Tame is doing something. I sense a change happening, something communal. I want to speak out for the other women who've endured this. No, it's more than that. I have to. There is a feeling of sisterhood here, and especially because it is about my creative life, and the career I have spent thirty years developing. This is my territory. Isolating women, the expectation that we'll compete against each other, it's a tired and worn-out narrative. The men he surrounds himself with have always idolised him. Turned their backs on the jealousy and misery. And in this world climate, to what end? Why inflict pain on yourself and others, over and over? Why leave such a trail of destruction when there are so many people genuinely suffering? The power of self-sabotage is hollow. I encircle myself with a fortress of mates, collaborators, writers, musicians. My ring of steel.

Yeah I look so fine but I feel so low

The week before I finally escape, he says he's busy at night trying to catch his art in a net. But as he attempts to capture and pin this creature down, as he watches what happens when he pulls the wings off, I cradle mine in open palms. I admire the beautiful colours and patterns, the soft shivers of its delicate body. I watch the wings emerge, dorsal-basking in the warm light. I watch it flutter off into the bright sky.

THAT SWEET PROMENADE

BRAM PRESSER

THAT SWEET PROMENADE

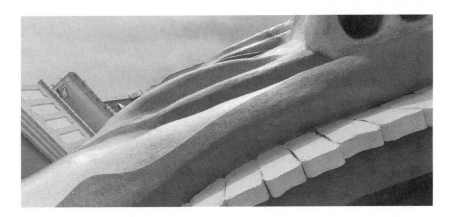

~ 1 ~

A cathedral of teeth.

He wakes and touches his finger to his lips; slides them into his mouth, prods at the gaps. He sucks, savours the sensation, a moment of pleasure. Around him St Kilda has come to life. Or he has come to life in St Kilda. She never sleeps. Never dies. He knows. He has always been here, a wanderer.

The clatter of a tram. Its unmistakable *ding*. Circus music.

The smell of popcorn and fairy floss. Screams as a train hurtles overhead on rickety tracks. Each time he wakes he asks himself, how has it not fallen?

People stream from all directions, expanding and contracting like breath, headed towards the golden castle. A strip of white above the doors, the name of a troubadour, a hometown boy, in bold block letters. They are here to welcome him back. Further down the Esplanade, there is a bridge where the troubadour once stood. Then, he was with a girl. On the stairs. They both wore black. She, a red beret. His hair was dark, tightly curled. It was a blustery day. They went to the pier, leaned on the railings as the water squalled beneath them. Nearby, a lonely saxophonist.

The wanderer remembers. He was there. Glimpsed as a flash on a screen, committed to video, lost to progress. How is it possible? He is mostly invisible. You don't notice him. But he was there. Watch the video. You will see.

He gathers his things and turns to the grass, the palm trees. He walks on to Acland Street.

~ 2 ~

You are already here.

You catch your reflection in the window as you stare at the cakes. You came as a child, with your grandmother and then, after she died *too young*, with your parents. For a while you brought your own children, though they have stopped coming. They have other plans. Friends. Anything other than being seen with you. It will change, you know, but for now it is just you, in front of the window, staring at the selection as if you haven't already decided. *Kugelhopf*, with its soft dough and thick, gooey innards. It is why you come. The dusting of chocolate powder that rims your nostrils and clings to your whiskers. You look up at the sign, *Monarch Cakes*, and remember your father; how he used to look up at it, too.

You live far away. *On the other side of town.* Summer draws you back, nights like these, when the sun is reluctant to set, and rests on an invisible hammock between the palms. Tonight, you are meeting a friend. He still lives nearby. The shopkeepers know him by name. You will dine at Cicciolina, then walk to the beach, take off your shoes and stand in the water. As waves lap at your ankles, you will talk about his treatment. You will try not to think it's the last time.

You volunteered to come early, put your name on the list and wait for a table. You've never understood a restaurant that doesn't take reservations. You have already been to the bookstore. There is time for cake, you think.

The strum of a guitar. You hadn't noticed the girl setting up. She puts a small hat on the ground by her feet. She looks around. A few people stop. They are holding cones with ice-cream that is already dripping onto their hands. The girl crouches and switches on a small amplifier. A few chords, some adjusting of the knobs, and she is ready. *Hi*, she says into the microphone. She looks past you, down the street, towards the Palais Theatre, where a concert is underway. She begins to sing.

About strangers.

And shows.

Your phone buzzes. Your table is ready. The cake will have to wait. You turn around and walk to the restaurant, while quickly typing a text message. You don't notice the man who drifts past, like a spirit. You don't know that you have almost bumped into him. You can't know that he is always here. Always has been. Your friend should arrive soon.

The girl is still singing.

About dreams.

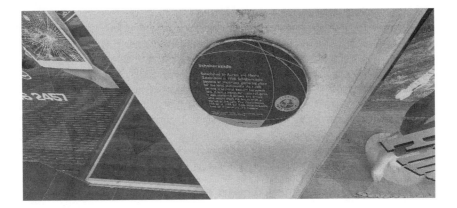

~ 3 ~

Night has fallen, the crowds have thinned.

The wanderer waits now for ghosts.

What once was here is all but forgotten, sacrificed to progress, to the economy, to fashion. He sits on a stone bollard and looks at the narrow strip of wall that separates sheets of painted glass. On it, a circle of blue with the name of a thousand and one stories. *Scheherazade*. It is, he knows, a portal, from which the ghosts will come, one by one, like they did all those years ago, before they were ghosts, through the door, to gather, to talk. A parliament of the haggard and the wise. They were the *luftmenschen*. People of the sky. They had landed on this earth, at this particular place, at that particular time, not by chance or choice. It was fate, first cruel, then kind. They met and they feasted and they talked and now they are gone. Returned to the clouds, from which they still descend some nights, to continue what they had left unfinished: to solve the world's problems. How little has changed; how tragic that their wisdom is still so desperately needed.

They are late. He stands and shuffles over to the bin, rummages for something to eat. Whatever he finds will remind him of those days. The food of the lost and dispossessed. Food that itself was home. Food through which their friends and family would once again be sitting at their table, though they were dining alone. A room of tables for one until it too became a community of sorts, and the place was packed with lost souls and outcasts, who were welcomed with joy by a man with bushy eyebrows.

He pulls a brown paper bag from the bin and unfurls its top. Inside there are chips. A napkin, too, smeared with tomato sauce and scrunched into a ball. He plucks out a chip and lays it on his tongue. He closes his eyes and his jaw clenches shut. Salty. And a little sweet. The sharpness of vinegar. Just like … He remembers the schnitzel, as big as a plate, that he once ate only a few steps from here.

Shmuel!

Jakub!

The wanderer opens his eyes. They are here, embracing one another. These two, but then more. The one called Shmuel recognises him, smiles and nods. He takes another chip from the bag. The coolness of sauce, smeared against his knuckle. He listens, as he does most nights, to the babble of words he does not know. Occasionally, there will be something familiar; a place, an event. But it has been changed, twisted ever so slightly on the contours of new tongues. They talk with their hands, wild gesticulations that give way to pats and pushes and, almost always, a warm hug.

One last ghost. The faintest of them all, for, somewhere far from here, there is someone who looks just like him, but older, alive, walking the streets. This ghost cannot glow like the others. He is not fully formed. It's something our man on the bollard has come to understand: we leave our former selves behind. While we live, the spectres of who we once were continue to haunt the places we've been. Only death calls them together, binds them in a single luminous form. The pale ghost is skittish. He clutches a notepad and pencil. He, too, stands a little apart from the rest. They call out to him, beckon for him to come closer.

Areleh! Nu?

The bag is empty and the scene begins to fade. The ghosts turn and step towards the wall. They become mist, sea breeze, tendrils that snake behind the blue circle and disappear. Only Shmuel remains. He shrugs at the man and raises his hand, palm facing forward. *Until next time.* And then Shmuel, too, is gone. The street is silent, the night completely still.

He wanders on. Time means nothing to him. It is there, like the tide.

~ **4** ~

You stand at the bar, an empty glass in your hand. It feels strange to be here again. Without him. To see how it's changed.

Sterilised.

Ossified.

You never made it to the beach. The conversation waned while you waited for dessert. Your friend was tired, he said. His face had thinned, his skin a dull grey. He poked limply at his sticky date pudding. You said goodbye on the corner of Acland and Carlisle streets. *We should do this again*, he said without irony. You offered to walk with him but he just smiled and waved his hand. *I'll be fine,* he said. *It was … this was nice,* you said. He started walking towards Barkly Street. You watched until he disappeared around the corner. And then you came here, to the small underground haven – The Public Bar – beneath the Esplanade Hotel. To be alone with your memories of him. Of that first night.

~

A tempest of flesh, bodies at war; heaving, tumbling, colliding in ecstasy. It is a conflagration. An orgy. Crushed together, you form a single mass, pulsing, convulsing, to spitfire blasts. You struggle to breathe, lock arms with your friend. Above, on a small platform, four ragged misfits, carnival freaks, thrash about, swinging their instruments, smashing them. A tangle of carnal rage. The mass surges forward, spilling over the invisible border, grasping at the misfits, drawing them in. A discordant boom; the bassist is wielding his guitar as a weapon, swinging at those who get too close. His toga has come loose, he is nearly naked, his skin scarred and etched. Still, the song continues. Jagged, distorted chords that warp the air, cleave a path through the sweaty haze. Clutching the microphone, the singer screams, indecipherable. His coloured dreadlocks whip around him. In his other hand, the twisted horn of a desert goat. He thrusts it skyward and the crowd cheers. It is ritual now, this moment. The singer lowers one end of the horn. He grins and light glints off the metal barbs in his face. Hands reach out, pull, snatch. He steps away from the microphone. All around, the storm rages on. A violent, euphoric swirl. He returns holding a bottle, tips it into the horn. More cheers, while those who can, guzzle. You friend passes you the spout. You suck, gag, spray out the rancid purple swill. The singer grabs the microphone again and continues to scream. You are all screaming, too, fists punching up, out. Something hurtles overhead. Thwack. A splatter of thick, brown sludge, across the drummer's face. He leaps over the kit, dives into the crowd. It opens like a mouth then closes back around him. Subsumed, consumed, in the bowels of this white stone monolith. And then he, too, is spat out, passed along overhead, between clenched fists, until he is dumped on a deserted stage. Guitars lean against squealing amps. The drummer, stinking of garlic and sacramental wine, oozing blood and sweat and maybe a drizzle of vomit, tucks in his knees, leans back on his arms and begins to laugh. Beside him, a single pot of beer, freshly poured.

∼

The walls still thrum; the faint echo of chaos. Stories. Songs.

Nothing can change that.

It's time you went home.

~ 5 ~

The scent of morning. Seaweed. Bacon.

He ducks to avoid the tassels that hang from the lintel and steps inside. This place is his anchor. Sometimes when the wanderer wakes, he does not recognise what is around him. Only the sounds of the ocean. A day has passed. A year. A decade. This is where he comes to centre himself, to know that he is not lost. Here, where nothing changes. Where there is no need for ghosts.

He rushes past the tables and locks himself in the toilet. Words fill the walls; names, jokes, drunken philosophy. He scans them for messages. For answers. He considers writing the question, but it does not come. He stands, flushes and leaves the stall. When he rounds the corner, he sees the café has filled. Familiar faces. Morning faces. Faces from the newspapers some use for shelter at night. They call to each other from across the room. He passes the register and sees a paper cup with a black plastic lid waiting on the bench. A crude stamp. An old sailing ship. The Galleon Café. He picks it up and cradles it between his palms. He turns to the woman at the coffee machine, but she looks away.

The door opens and a man enters, followed by a little girl. Father and daughter. He has seen them many times before. They are locals. Regulars. The father is dishevelled, as always; his jeans and jacket stained, his t-shirt faded, his hair hanging in dirty knots that reach to his knees. Knots that once gleamed with incandescent colour. The girl is impeccable; a smart, red coat buttoned to the neck, shoes with lights that twinkle with each step, blonde curls pulled back into a high ponytail. He remembers when she was a baby, when the father and the girl's mother brought her in a bassinet and placed her on the table for all to see. They had come straight from the hospital. The girl was a few days old. She was going home. But first, here. A rush from behind the counter to see, to hold.

What did you call her?

We don't know yet.

She must be four now. Maybe five. They still make a fuss, like she is their own. A waitress directs them to a round table near the register. *Their table.* Once they are seated, the waitress comes over. Then another. They kneel next to the little girl. She shows them a book with stickers and activities. She says *Actiwities.* Or she did. He doesn't remember when that stopped. A waiter in a baseball cap, his jeans hitched too high, joins them.

What ya havin'?

The wanderer takes a sip of coffee. He can recite their order by heart. For the father: *Half serve poached eggs, no butter, eggs on the side, with a side of mushrooms and spinach.* For the girl: *Eggies and cheese.* If the mother is there: *Oat chai, the old one. And pancakes.* But today she is not.

The father is looking at his phone. A game. It usually is. The girl is colouring her pages. She stops, lost in thought, then puts down her pencil.

Daddy?

The father looks up.

Only oceans know language.

The wanderer takes another sip of coffee and makes his way to the entrance. He should write that on the toilet wall, he thinks. Before he forgets. But he is already gone.

~ **6** ~

When you wake, she has left to start her day. There is a note beside you.

You cried in you sleep. Call me. Xx.

You reach across and grab your phone, hoping for a message. That he is okay. That he enjoyed the night. That it wasn't just a dream. That it was. You dread what will one day come. You begin to write something, then delete it.

You think of that sweet promenade. Of your parents and friends. The sea, the sand, the hills of grass. The pavement, the windows, the painted alleys. The ghosts, the smoke, the broken bottles. Street walkers, drug dealers, rough sleepers. The thrust of bodies. Violence, despair. Laughter.

The crackle of static where worlds collide.

You dial her number and wait.

SPECIAL TREATMENT

GINA WILLIAMS

SPECIAL TREATMENT

We were sitting in my friend's flat in Darwin, four of us on chrome-and-sky-blue chairs around a pale blue Laminex table, trying to catch a bit of moving air. It was summertime, and the overhead fan was valiantly fighting to create warm zephyrs in this tiny space.

If you could strategically place yourself underneath its dusty blades, you might not feel cool, but at least you could feel some movement of air. At this time of year, it's the stillness of the air that's just as oppressive as the baking heat.

There was me, my friend Terry, his daughter and a middle-aged woman who was an old friend of Terry's.

It was 1989 and there was a national pilots' strike and I was stranded, trying to make my way back home to Perth from Sydney. Darwin was my closest port to WA, and I figured if I could get there, then at least I only had one border to cross and I could hitchhike or try to grab a cheap bus ticket home.

Terry had invited me to come camp for a couple of days while I sorted myself out. I was running out of time and money, so his kind gesture was gratefully received.

Middle-Aged Lady, sitting across from me, strenuously objected to me being there, elbow resting on the table while her finger wiggled and pointed at me, telling me in no uncertain terms I wasn't welcome, there was no room and I needed to move on, but Terry wasn't having a bar of that.

He took her aside to the kitchen, about three metres away as though that was going to give them some kind of privacy while he told her in a low growl, 'MY house, I'VE invited her, and she can stay as long as she wants!'

Daughter and I turned away, pretending not to notice the exchange.

Gawd. How awkward.

They returned to the table, and we sat in this horrible, uncomfortable silence.

Looking around, Terry suddenly perked up with an idea.

'Bub, why don't you sing us a song!' He motioned to his daughter to pick up her guitar in the corner of the room. Keen to break the tension, she leapt up and grabbed the instrument, sliding back into her seat, explaining as she strummed and tweaked the strings, trying to nudge them into tune, that this wasn't her song, this was a Paul Kelly song.

Good grief, I thought, *here we go ... another one of those earnest tales of Australia, where all the relationships start out rocky, then rapidly turn to shit from there. You either end up in jail or on the streets or staring at the bottom of a glass, and we all cry in our beers at the sheer bloody misery of it all ...* Mind you, after what had just transpired, I was sure this would come as a bit of comic relief.

And then she sang.

'Grandfather walked this land in chains, a land he called his own ...'

The words struck something deep, something painful in my heart, and I found myself catching my breath. My first response of course was cranky and defensive: who was this little girl? Who was this little blonde slip of a thing, singing these words, written by a complete stranger? She didn't know my story, how on earth could she? And him!!! How could he write something like this? How could he know?

'He was given, another name, and taken into town …'

I sat there, the back of my throat feeling tight and burning, blinking furiously so my eyes wouldn't betray my emotions.

I'd only recently found and been reunited with my biological mother and family. Given another name? Everything was raw. Everything was a revelation. My birth name was Laurel Lee, and I was given the name Gina by my adoptive parents.

I didn't know anything about my biological family at the time – I was just at the beginning of a whole journey of discovery around who I was, where I was from and who my mob were. Because in our community, that's what's important. Your connection is what really counts.

Verse by verse, this song seemed to be reading my mail. The biggest sting came (of course) in the tail, the last verse.

I never spoke my mother's tongue
I never knew my name
I never learnt the songs she sung
I was raised in shame

The song ended, everyone clapped. I just sat there, face burning, waiting for the right moment to excuse myself. It was a strange feeling, listening to the words, I remember feeling embarrassed. I was sitting at this table, the only Aboriginal person, and everyone else in the room seemed to know more about my history, my nation's history, than I did.

I felt shame.

Snappy-pointy-finger-lady was suddenly caught up in the beauty of the moment, and she blurted out an apology directed at me.

'Of course you should stay,' she said, smiling, 'you should stay as long as you want, it is the least we can do after all.'

I felt ill. A feeble 'thanks' was as much as I could muster.

For days that song rattled around in my head, all the way back to Perth and, in the weeks that followed, I kept thinking about it, turning the lyrics over and over. I bought a cassette of the album *Building Bridges*, a compilation album that included the song, and played it over and over until the tape eventually snapped.

To this day, I can still hear Paul Kelly's humble introduction, 'I hear a lot of people say that blackfullas in this … ah … blackfullas getting a lot of special treatment in this country so I thought I'd write a song about it …'

The guitar strums, then his voice calls out … earnestly of course, but beautiful and powerful and poignant nonetheless.

The emotions I'd attached to these lyrics and the song started somewhere in deep sadness, then somehow managed to drift into rage and indignation, until finally, they gently landed on a simple grief.

Except that grief is never simple, or gentle.

The months turned into years and every now and then, when I'd hear that song, always it took me back to that sweaty room in Darwin.

Always, I would feel that familiar, dull ache in my chest. Sometimes I didn't even need to hear the song, something would happen, or someone would say something, and it would conjure this memory, and suddenly I would be sat back with these feelings … these raw feelings.

Working in media, sitting in court as a junior reporter, listening to people telling their stories, defending themselves as part of the Royal Commission into Aboriginal Deaths in Custody always managed to bring this song to mind. One case, a man who was incarcerated, complained of chest pains. Prison officers essentially ran with him back and forth from his cell to a waiting vehicle to transfer him to hospital. He died of a massive heart attack. Nobody was charged.

He got special treatment.

Being in Sydney on work experience and being sent with another reporter to the funeral of a police officer who died from injuries he sustained during a police raid where an unarmed Aboriginal man was shot and killed while his nine-year-old son slept in the room next door.

The police officer was buried a hero.

The twenty-nine-year-old Aboriginal man who had broken no laws, yet died in an unlawful raid was eventually recognised as a death in custody.

He got special treatment.

Being on the receiving end of vile name-calling from nameless racists who don't care who sees their tirades, even if that witness happens to be your four-year-old son sitting in the car waiting for you to buckle him in.

Or worse, well-meaning people asking me 'What part Aboriginal are you? It's just that … you don't look it; you could pass off as anything.'

For the longest time I couldn't answer, because I simply didn't know. I didn't know my history. And talking to other Noongar people, hearing their howls of protest, 'They can't ask that! What do they mean, what part? Your foot?' I learned quickly not to engage with that on any side of the debate. A dear friend eventually said it was more like being a 'cup of tea,' because 'you can put milk in tea but it's still tea. Really it comes down to this; you either identify as Aboriginal or you don't.'

I did. I identified. And I got special treatment.

As I continued to work and grow in the media as a reporter, the consistent theme was that I'd 'obviously had the benefit of a good upbringing'. Which was true, I had. But I never had the opportunity to define that, because it wasn't what you'd naturally consider to be a 'good upbringing'.

I was adopted as a baby to Aboriginal people who didn't identify as such. My dad all but turned his back on his Indigeneity, which I now realise was because he was raised in shame.

He got special treatment.

When my adoptive dad passed, the courts decided my mother (who was clearly sick with alcoholism) needed to be given the opportunity to prove herself an unfit mother because I couldn't be proven to be an uncontrollable child. So, as a twelve-year-old, I was placed in a house where trauma and domestic violence and substance abuse became the norm.

I got special treatment.

Two foster homes later, I discovered I was adopted and started looking for my family. My biological mother had been taken away as a seven-year-old and placed on a mission. She was told her family didn't want her. She was told her family was dead. She had Noongar language beaten from her. She was told she would never leave the mission. She believed this.

She got special treatment.

Her mother, my grandmother, was born on Gitja country, in the East Kimberley of Western Australia. Her parents had moved her and her sister around the region, trying to keep the family together. Eventually they landed at Moola Bulla Station outside of Halls Creek, and as a four-year-old, she was marched 580 km from Moola Bulla to Derby, where they transferred her to Carrolup mission.

In later years she was moved to the notorious Moore River Native Settlement where they sent her out to work as a domestic servant for various nyidiyung (white) families. She kept running away, her notes say at one point she lacked the intelligence to stay put, so should be brought back into the custody of the mission, dead or alive.

She got special treatment.

Of course, there was also a lot of goodness in my life, working on a regional television program, *Milbindi*, which focused on the positive achievements and aspirations of Aboriginal people in Western Australia, and continued to highlight the amazing stuff that abounded in our community.

And personally, a lot of people who stepped up and helped me in my pursuit to claw back what was lost were generous and kind.

But overwhelmingly, even when I was reporting positive news, I found almost everyone I encountered seemed to have a story attached to Stolen Generations, to deaths in custody, to separation of families, removal from heartlands and removal of language.

Removal of language is especially devastating, because you cannot separate language from culture.

They got special treatment.

Many years later, when a full circle brought me back to working at Noongar Radio, I made an attempt to find out more about my adoptive father. Until he passed, he had been the centre of my universe. I wondered what happened to make him turn his back on community like he did, and I thought perhaps his Native Welfare records might offer some insight.

I contacted the records bureau to try to access his records and piece together his story. He had a small file, less than thirty pages. I felt hopeful, but the conversation ended abruptly when I was informed that because I was adopted, I had no rights to his records. I needed to seek permission from a biologically connected relative.

'But I don't know anyone! He never talked about his family or his history,' I begged down the phone. 'Please, this man held no office and he broke no laws. He did nothing remarkable, except he chose me. Please help me to understand what happened to him. Please, please don't do this, it's cruel.'

The faceless bureaucrat sighed down the line. 'Look I'm really sorry, but these are the rules and there's nothing I can offer you here. You will need to obtain the signature of a close relative. I can't give you any names, you will have to try and work it out. I'm really sorry.' And with that she hung up.

We got special treatment.

In 2009, I enrolled in a Noongar language course run by a local TAFE. I was nervous and excited and hoped that by learning Language I might be able to glue some pieces together. By this stage, I knew my family, where I was from, but I never spoke my mother's tongue. I'd been raised in shame.

I was the only Noongar in the room, and when asked what I was doing there I sprang out like a bull out of a gate, loudly declaring that I was 'shamed that I had to come to TAFE to learn something that should have been my birthright.

Another lady in the room spoke. 'That's not your shame, that's ours.'

When asked again what I was doing there, without even thinking I answered, 'I want to write songs in Language, and I want to sing Language.'

I want to sing my mother's tongue ...

For the first time, there appeared to be an opportunity to respond to this song that had burned itself on my heart in such a profound way. Maybe, just maybe I might be able to rewrite that final stinging verse.

In the years that followed, many songs in Noongar language have been written, and in turn I have become able to fluently speak (and sing) my Language. More importantly, other Noongar artists, performers, poets, writers and dreamers have stepped up and started doing the same thing. It's a beautiful thing.

And a couple of months ago, in a strange twist of events, I found myself having a chance conversation with an acquaintance who worked with research and helping people access Aboriginal family history records. I scoffed at the time, relating my story of being shut down and denied any access at all to my adopted father's records because of my status as an adoptee.

'Oh, I think you can get some information, I think you will find it's managed under a different structure now and things have changed,' he quickly assured me.

My heart leapt a little, though I felt sceptical. Still, we exchanged numbers and went our separate ways. By the end of that afternoon, I received a text message, followed by an email and some forms to fill in. I quickly responded and held my breath.

The first message arrived, telling me they had found my dad's file. I sat there, in tears as it all started to unfold.

Grandfather walked this land in chains …

Actually, no, he didn't. There was so much more to that story. The records showed my adopted dad was descended from Noongar royalty. His great-great-great-great grandparents were Tulbich (King Onion) and Ngaiyongart from Wardarndi country in the south-west.

There was an article in the newspaper where Tulbich sent a telegram to John Forrest, asking for a train ticket from Bunbury to Perth. Forrest wrote back, telling him he talked too much, he smelled bad and would be a nuisance to the other passengers.

More telling though was dad's mother – my grandmother Maggie – who worked as a domestic servant for A.O. Neville. She ran away and ended up in Quairading, in the Wheatbelt of WA. Funny enough, that's also where my biological family are connected.

But most heartbreaking was the single page, a letter to Sister Kate from the Commissioner for Native Affairs, asking her to take my father in, describing him as a 'nice child'.

Even now, this description of my dad makes me weep.

As more and more information has come through about both my biological and adopted families, I have found myself slowly starting to heal. Empowered by the words of the poets, we find ourselves able to start rewriting these scripts.

Nowadays I find myself singing this song out of victory rather than grief. And, with great respect, I added a small language stanza to the end of Mr Kelly's incredible, powerful verse:

Ngany moort boodja wumbadiny koorl
My family walked the land with pride
Ngalang boodjara
Our land
Koora koora, yeyi, benang
Past, present, future
Noongar boodjara
Noongar land

Ngalak moorditj moortung
We are strong people
Ngalak wumbadiny moortung
We are proud people
Kwobba Noongar moortung
Beautiful Noongar people

GOD TOLD ME TO

MATT NEAL

GOD TOLD ME TO

The first two lines of 'God Told Me To' pull off one of my favourite daredevil rhymes. Straight out of the blocks, within seconds of introducing his murderous protagonist, John Johanna, Paul Kelly rhymes 'misunderstood' with 'blood'. In my broad son-of-a-dairy-farmer accent, it's barely a half-rhyme. In Kelly's laconic delivery … yeah, it's still barely a half-rhyme.

It's not quite in my top tier of sleight-of-hand rhyming. Those key positions are reserved for when Arctic Monkeys' Alex Turner rhymes 'something' with 'stomach' in 'When the Sun Goes Down', courtesy of his Sheffieldian pronunciation of 'something' as 'summat'. Or when XTC's Andy Partridge bends the English language to his whim in 'Season Cycle' to rhyme 'cycle' with 'umbilical'. Or when Wayne Cohen of The Flaming Lips does the impossible and rhymes 'orange' with 'store' in 'She Don't Use Jelly', a feat all the more remarkable because I have a rhyming dictionary on my desk that's literally titled *Nothing Rhymes With Orange*.

Kelly's misunderstood/blood couplet isn't as daring as any of these, but it's still up there in terms of highwire half-rhymes. Maybe top ten. Doing it in the opening couplet is definitely cheeky. It's the kind of rhyme you can only pull off with certainty when you're eighteen albums into your career.

Of course, this is probably the least significant or noteworthy thing about 'God Told Me To', but most of the significant or noteworthy things relate to deep shit, like religion. I thought it prudent to butter you up with something less serious before we dive in. I mean, you start the dinner party off with small talk and a bottle and a half of red before you bring up things like religion, right?

'God Told Me To', a song unlike any other in his back catalogue, is off Paul Kelly's 2007 album *Stolen Apples*, which came out at a fascinating time in his career. It was his first 'normal' album since 2001's … *Nothing but a Dream*, and sits at the tail end of a remarkable stretch of experimentation. After *Stolen Apples*, it would be five years before he made another record, having smashed out eight albums and heavily contributed to seven soundtracks between 1998 and 2007. This makes *Stolen Apples* the familiar dessert at the end of a very eclectic degustation; the exclamation mark on a strange yet captivating paragraph.

This era of exploration started in 1999 with two simultaneously released albums that could not have been more different – a bluegrass album titled *Smoke* (recorded with Melbourne band Uncle Bill) and the jam-heavy grooves of the self-titled album from Professor Ratbaggy (a project formed with three members of his regular backing band). Kelly then drifted through the sprawling double album *Ways & Means* (a double album being something of an experiment after 1979), an album of joyous tongue-in-cheek cabaret band-vibes as part of Melbourne 'supergroup' Stardust Five, and another bluegrass album (*Foggy Highway*). In between, he had a hand in the soundtracks for a short film (*Big House*), feature films (*Lantana, Silent Partner, Tom White* and *Jindabyne*), an in-between film (*One Night the Moon*, in which he also starred) and a TV series (*Fireflies*).

There are a couple of straight-up Kelly albums amid the experimentation, but even those have their way-out-of-left-field moments: check out the late nineties electronica influence in the double shot of 'Just About to Break' and the underrated 'Love is the Law', both tucked away in the middle of his album … *Nothing but a Dream*. If you only know Paul Kelly for 'To Her Door' and 'How to Make Gravy', those tunes will surprise you like a mugger in a Melbourne alley.

To his record label, *Stolen Apples* must've seemed like the fast bowler coming back on with the new ball after the captain's tried to get a wicket out of everyone but the wicketkeeper. There are still moments of experimentation on it – the brilliant opener 'Feelings of Grief' sounds more like Kelly fronting American band Explosions in the Sky than your typical PK offering, for instance – but the explorations are tame compared to the Professor Ratbaggy stuff or songs like 'Just About to Break'.

But among an album of quality material, 'God Told Me To' is on a whole other level. Like so many great songs, it starts with a howl of feedback – think The Beatles' 'I Feel Fine', Hendrix's 'Foxey Lady', Tool's 'Sober', Bowie's 'The Width of a Circle' and Sleater-Kinney's 'The Fox'. Feedback is always an excellent way to start a song. It sounds like chaos and lightning, and it's one of the most fun things you can do with an electric guitar. Feedback is like a brumby – it's wild and unhinged, but when you learn how to tame it, you can

Man-From-Snowy-River that shit right down the side of a bloody mountain.

In this case, the feedback (courtesy of Kelly's nephew Dan, a masterful songwriter in his own right) is a howl of furious biblical anger, as it opens the tale of the aforementioned John Johanna – a murderer who has more than likely killed in the name of his God. He sees wickedness all around him and considers his acts as 'most righteous'. John is fighting his own private holy war against Satan, wielding a holy fire as he goes, powered by angels, his anger a weapon with which to smite the infidels.

Have you had that bottle and a half of red yet? Good, 'cos we're gonna talk about religion.

I've heard some people refer to *Stolen Apples* as Kelly's 'religious album', but it's religious in the same way that devil-worshipping is religious. Titles like 'The Lion and the Lamb', 'Stolen Apples Taste the Sweetest' and 'God Told Me To' hint at furtive bible studies during the album's writing, but they're misdirections. 'The Lion and the Lamb' is a song of self-affirmation, 'Stolen Apples Taste the Sweetest' is a barely disguised ode to an affair, and 'God Told Me To' is about a killer, as told from the killer's perspective. Chuck in the lascivious track 'Right Outta My Head' (key lyric: 'I'm gonna fuck her right outta my head'), and this record will get you chucked out of Sunday School. People like to refer to Paul Kelly as Australia's Bob Dylan, but when Bob Dylan did a religious album, he became a born-again preacher. When Paul Kelly did it, he drew a pentagram on the floor and started looking for nuns to hook up with.

John Johanna, with his God-given blood-soaked calling, is one of the most fascinating characters in the Kelly canon. While not as nuanced as, say, the married-too-early couple of 'To Her Door', or jailbird Joe from 'How to Make Gravy', he's still intriguing. Who is he? Where's he going? What's he done? And most importantly, what's he going to do next? These are questions that flood my brain every time I hear this song.

That fantastic barely-half-rhyme opening couplet is laden with suggestion:

'My name is John Johanna, I am misunderstood
Lately, I have been accused of grievous murder in cold blood.'

This is the start of his sermon, but like any screenwriter worth his salt, Kelly has employed the first half of one of screenwriting's golden rules: 'enter late, leave early'. The alleged incident has already occurred. But how did this murder happen? Who did he kill? How recent is 'lately'? Tell me, dammit!

Kelly really digs into the screenwriting tricks. John Johanna doesn't admit to doing anything wrong – he just points out he's been accused. Good: keep the audience guessing. But where is John Johanna making this sermon? This is a trick songwriters can use more easily than screenwriters. Every scene in a script starts with a location – 'Exterior. Swamp. Day.' as Dr Teeth puts it in a wonderfully meta-moment in *The Muppet Movie*. Songwriters don't have to do that sort of thing. They just barrel in with four chords and the truth, locations be damned.

So is John Johanna in jail? In the dock of a courtroom? Perhaps, like the hapless Walter Neff in the classic Billy Wilder film *Double Indemnity*, he's intoning his message into a dictaphone while bleeding from a gut wound. Or maybe he's standing on a street corner in the Melbourne CBD, yelling stridently over the sound of the traffic, wearing a sandwich board that reads *Repent – The End Is Nigh*.

John Johanna doesn't admit his guilt, but as you surge on to the second half of the first verse, you get the feeling he's as guilty as a billionaire living in a tax haven:

> 'My mission is most righteous, my cause is true and just
> The wicked need chastisement, you know it's either them or us.'

Firstly, kudos for getting the word 'chastisement' into a rock song, Mr Kelly. Secondly, the longer the song goes on, the crazier John Johanna gets. The telltale signs are adding up in the first verse, but by the time we get to the second verse, John sees Satan gathering his forces in broad daylight, and likens his own anger to a holy hammer. By the third and final verse, he's gone full Revelation (never go full Revelation), invoking all kinds of esoteric imagery – seven golden candles, a two-edged sword, seven stars and a beast of many eyes. I have no idea what all that means and I'm too frightened to find out.

And in between it all, John Johanna tells us he did what he had to do because God told him to. The harmonies on the final 'God told me to' of each chorus resound like the voices in John Johanna's own head. By this point, we've forgotten the accusations of murder and are just hoping this fella gets the help he needs, preferably in a location a long way away from the general public.

The line that's hit me the hardest and has stuck with me the most over the years arrives at the tail of the last verse: 'Those not with me are against me'. When I first heard this song in 2007 (on national youth broadcaster triple j, where it was on medium rotation, believe it or not) I was not aware of that line's biblical roots, or that it had been used by everyone from Cicero to Orwell to Mussolini.

I only knew of it from George W. Bush, who invoked its sentiments in the days following September 11, some six years prior to the release of 'God Told Me To': 'Either you are with us, or you are with the terrorists'. (Sidenote: Hillary Clinton used a very similar line two days after September 11, so there was a fair bit of this us-vs-them-ism going around at that point in time.)

For right or wrong, linking the song in my head to George Dubya and his subsequent War on Terror unlocked the true levels of genius in Kelly's song for me. And it seems that was Kelly's intention. He told journalist Michael Dwyer in an interview for *The Age* in 2007 that he'd lifted the last verse straight out of Revelation, adding for good measure that this was the bit of the Bible favoured by fundamental Christians such as Bush and America's religious right. As a cherry on top, Kelly noted they were a similar level of crazy to fundamentalist Islamists. Same shit, different bucket, so to speak.

'God Told Me To' arrived in a world where Muslim extremists waged jihad and the Christian West rose to meet it by invading oil-rich countries. Anti-Islamic sentiment bubbled away all around the world, and the Americans beating the war drums draped themselves in flags and clutched bibles to their chests. In this climate, John Johanna's dividing line of 'those not with me are against me' felt all too real – like something off the very same 6.30 news where Skyhooks saw their horror movie.

And all of a sudden, John Johanna wasn't just a crazy killer ranting on the corner of Bourke and Elizabeth – in my mind, he became every person who had ever done horrible things in the name of religion. He was every leader sending their troops to war against the infidels. He was every king launching a crusade, he was every abortion clinic bomber, he was every homophobe beating a gay person, he was every executioner beheading blasphemers in a soccer stadium … all because their god told them to.

Writing songs denouncing the perversion or misappropriation of religion is difficult. Believe me, I know, I've tried. XTC's 'Dear God' nails it, taking the old (weird) idea of a kid's letter to God and spinning it into a line of questioning about how almighty the Almighty really is if they let people starve/drown/die of disease. It's ingeniously incisive while also having a sense of drama and being as catchy as corona.

Kelly tackles similarly deep shit in 'God Told Me To', but as a character study – something he excels at. It's a very Paul Kelly way to write a song that's very un–Paul Kelly–like.

But it's songs like 'God Told Me To' that make me admire Kelly on a whole other level – he's so daring, and I find that impressive. That he can write something as achingly beautiful and straight-ahead as 'When I First Met Your Ma' and then turn around and write something as violently pointed as 'God Told Me To' – and that both songs are great – is astounding. It's the same level of musical courage that sees him do something like Professor Ratbaggy or a couple of bluegrass records or a mini-album of Shakespeare sonnets or a couple of experimental electro-rock songs in the middle of an otherwise 'normal' solo album.

It's the same kind of bravado that lets him dare to rhyme 'misunderstood' with 'blood'. Cheeky sod.

WAKE

SAM CARMODY

WAKE

Fred was awake at four thirty. A swimmer's habit. Not to wake with the sun, but before it. At least when she hadn't overdone the night before. There was something Catholic about her habits, she knew. Saved or damned.

Her bathers were still wet, cool on her skin. Could smell the sea on them. Grains of beach sand in the seams.

She filled her water bottle at the sink. Moonlight on the kitchen table. Went briskly through the quiet dark of the living room. Held her breath when she walked through there. Every time, even in daylight, as silly as that was, of course. Never looked to the space of carpet near the balcony doors, as if she might see Rob, a shadow outstretched on the hospital bed, silhouetted by the moon.

Rob first noticed the growth on a long weekend in Busselton. Fred was lying on the hotel bed when he came out of the bathroom suite, about to shower after their swim. Produced his scrotum looking all angry on one side, one testicle swollen. Rob thought it could have been the heat, or bad pool water. Some sort of infection. Fred had felt it. Through the skin it felt unnaturally hard. Rob saw the GP as soon as they got back to Perth, was having an ultrasound that afternoon. He was in hospital two days later.

After the surgery she would often find him poking his half-full scrotum, standing in front of the bathroom mirror or the long mirror in the clothes cupboard, hunched over his naked body. Had the look as if he was trying to gently wake something, or someone, index finger out, tenderly touching it.

It was a short walk from the apartment. She went barefoot over the wind-worn bitumen to the footpath, then took the stairs down to the sand. The beach purplish in the low light.

Fred couldn't speak of it. When they first found out she'd kept it to herself. Even caught herself lying, which was an alien act to her. The truth came easily to Fred, even hard truths. Particularly hard truths. But this. She felt the tight seal on it all. The lockdown that was happening beyond her conscious mind. A security measure acting beyond her control.

She'd blurted to a chemist one day that her husband was sick, and felt her body tense. Stood there, tears welling, mute as a child. Knew the discomfort of the pharmacist, a messy-haired man in his early thirties who would look more at home behind the counter of a surf shop.

I'm sorry, he said.

She'd shaken her head.

The first few strokes, it was the shock of the cold, of holding breath. The stimulus of immersion. Body adrenalised, the heart going, and trying to settle it all down. Fred liked this. That awareness of breath.

Of body. The pleasure of gaining control of your nervous system, like a pilot controlling a freefall.

He had radiotherapy. They hadn't got the cancer as early as the surgeon was comfortable with. They'd throw everything at it they could.

After the initial diagnosis, Rob spoke of the cancer not as an enemy but in diplomatic clichés. It was a wake-up call. A blessing in disguise.

In Fred's mind the cancer was the unhinged villain of a comic book. Leery and unpredictable. Stalking the life they had, quietly threatening to take it all. They had never really spoken to each other about what they believed. About faith or an afterlife or whatever. It had been an unnecessary question, philosophical ground you covered in high school with teenage lovers, maybe. Perhaps they both assumed the atheism of the other. Now, with death in their face, the subject of the potential end of a life seemed like an intellectual blindspot, something they had overlooked. And something that, now it couldn't be avoided, rendered them awestruck, almost childlike.

In a hundred metres, her muscles were warm. Breath easy. An almost sleepy rhythm.

A stingray kited over the sand. A school of sweetlip, six or seven, emerged from underneath an overhang of reef.

She loved the procedural quiet of the seabed, the soundless organisation. Like a monastery, or the reading room of a city library. Everything seemed largely unbothered by her, indifferent to her presence at the surface. But not in a negative way. She felt small in the sea, yes. Incidental. But not insignificant. In a weird way, she felt welcome.

Rob took himself to some Buddhist night classes, and Fred had come along. Each class cost six dollars, held at a women's health clinic after hours. A dozen people in a room, listening to pre-recorded Dharma teachings, followed by meditation. Rob often fell asleep in those classes. Fred did too, tired from a day's work, and the administrative onslaught that a serious illness brought with it. The endless appointments. Phone calls with insurers. Keeping family at bay.

There was the time, too, that Fred had arranged a session with a Buddhist meditation teacher, at a temple in the hills north-east of the city. After the hour's drive they were met at the door of a temple by a bald-headed woman in an orange robe. She had a thin, pale face that reminded Fred of her own mother's, albeit without hair.

I told you on the phone you should come to an orientation session first, she said, and produced a hard smile, one that looked as if it'd been carved with force and difficulty, like an engraving on a school desk. Beyond her, inside the temple, a group lounged on rubber mats or pillows, stretching or sitting straight-backed on the floor. All harem pants and undercuts.

Yes, Fred had admitted. You did.

But you have come anyway.

Fred had wondered of the woman's life before the orange robe. Middle management, perhaps. A banker.

We've meditated before, Fred said. I just figured we would come sit in on the class.

What meditation have you done?

Ah, we've gone to classes, Rob had said, smiling apologetically. In Perth.

No, what meditation?

Gosh, Rob said, scratching his own newly bald head. Transcendental? he said, turning to Fred. Is that what it's called?

You will need to come to an orientation, the woman said, nodding. You will disrupt the class. I'm sorry you have driven all this way.

Fred had felt Rob's hand on her back, as if he could sense trouble brewing. She looked at the group on the floor of the temple who moments before she had envied in some way, but now they just looked preening and mean to her. And this woman in the robe, the certitude on her face. The delight she took in turning them away. Rob looked hurt, despite his smile. It wasn't difficult to injure him, and Fred could have punched the teacher right in her enlightened face.

At some point, Rob had let the night classes go. The prayer sung to the Dalai Lama, there was the stink of Church in it, which he'd weathered twelve years of, as Fred had. The Catholic school alumni were often like people who had just cleaned their hands in a public bathroom. They had an unwillingness to touch anything spiritual, broached philosophical doors with their shoulders and elbows. They had paid their dues.

And at first, he didn't seem to want God to save him.

But then they'd found cancer in his liver. His kidney. Rob took indefinite leave from the courts and began chemotherapy.

It wasn't so much that he wanted to be saved, Fred had come to think, or that he thought a miracle would come. Not at the end. The doctors had been unequivocal. The palliative nurses that visited were so kind and warm, but had no patience for fantasy. When Fred had cautiously brought up a new treatment she read about online, a Kenyan tamarind fruit extract, a nurse had herded her out onto the patio, fixed her with a serious expression. Told her she had seen too many people waste time, and time wasn't on Rob's side.

A recurring dream she had was the two of them swimming together. More memory than dream. Glancing off to her right often between breaths. See Rob, his pale body almost luminescent. Make sure she was matching his strokes, not getting too far ahead of him.

He worked hard for the mile they would swim, earned every metre. Rob's swimming style was one that seemed to encourage its critics to poetry. A coach had once said he was all enthusiasm, no technique. Another said he went through the water like a battering ram. Fred often thought he swam like a sea horse, bent at the hips, his long legs too low in the water. He took up swimming because of her. He couldn't even freestyle fifty metres in the pool the first time they met.

In her dream they would move over a sandy bottom, close to shore. Fred documenting the kinds of things that Rob would miss, swimming along behind her. A shovelnose ray with its sharklike tail, shuffling itself under the sand. An octopus tiptoeing across the shelf, like a cartoon burglar, before tucking its orange-red tentacles to fall headfirst into a hole in the reef.

On their last swim together, Fred had shot off, as she did. And as usual, realised too late that he was lagging behind. When she turned, she'd seen him at the surface, goggles off, looking around him like a man overboard. Or perhaps more like a child.

She had swum him to shore, Rob on his back, her arm across his bony chest.

Fuck, sorry Freddy. Sorry.

That face stayed with her. Pale, gaunt. A dark sea around him.

From then on, he'd come down to the water. Stood there on the beach, in a jumper and jeans, regardless of the heat. Or sat on the sand, on a towel, like her mother had done when she was a teen at surf-club meets.

She hadn't got around yet to moving on his things. Instead, she sort of danced around them. The bath towel he used, the colour of a golden retriever, she left sitting alone in the linen cabinet, even when it was the only clean thing she had. To put her face in it, to hold it around her body. It was an intimacy that felt wrong now. But of course, there was no throwing it out.

A person leaves so much of themselves, even when they don't intend to. The detritus of a body. She wondered how much of him was in the dust around the house. Occasionally she found his dark hairs at the base of the shower, tangled up in all the black, grimy shit in between the tiny tiles, or built up in the corners.

She braced herself every time she entered the living room, where the bed had been. Big hospital thing. The oxygen machine.

Fred and Rob had driven down the coast on Friday after work for an ocean swim event at Busselton on Saturday. A small meet held by the surf club. Stayed in a twin room at a hostel. They had sat in the small garden with backpackers ten or fifteen years younger than them, enjoying the vacuous conversation. Debating the appropriate degree of pubic hair on men and women. The virtues of pegging, which Fred hadn't heard of. They shared the joint of a Swedish kiteboarder named Magnus. Went back to the room mildly stoned and fucked giddily on the bed.

They woke to a strong westerly, the surface of the sea pulled taut, like a nurse-made bed. The sun still low, its light not yet in the water but glancing off it. Glary.

The swim was just a mile long. The course a simple there-and-back, parallel to the shore, but the markers set some distance out. Rob didn't mention it but she knew what he was thinking. Why did it have to be so far out?

He had looked alright as they waded out with the other swimmers. A ragged assortment of bodies and abilities. Leather-backed veterans. Surf-club teens squealing and shouting at one another in mock terror.

Fred saw Rob look shoreward, like a climber looking down at a canyon floor.

The gun went and the pack set off in a frenzy, adrenalised, like spooked cattle. Fred began slowly so Rob could follow her feet.

She was several hundred metres into the swim, near the buoys, when she realised he was no longer with her. She looked back, over the churn of swimmers behind her, scanned to the beach, and saw someone standing on the shore. Hands on knees. Rob.

He had panicked, he said later, embarrassed, but honest as always. It had all got to him. The roiling sea. The dark water he had glimpsed each time he had turned his head to the horizon to breathe. An eagle ray that shot across the seabed beneath him. He had copped an arm across the temple, too, hard but not enough to stun him, yet it had shaken him in a way he couldn't account for.

He couldn't breathe out into the water. Something was stopping him. Like he didn't want to disturb something. Make his presence known.

He started breaststroke, trying to settle his breath, his limbs. But then he was falling behind the pack, in the unsettled water of their wake. Alone.

When they got back to the lodge late morning, they made love again, but she could see the doubt on his face.

Afterward he admitted it, the failure he felt. As a man. Ashamed, and ashamed, too, that he would feel that way. Emasculated.

Then he'd gone to the shower and Fred had fallen asleep. She woke again to him standing at the end of the bed. Naked, holding his scrotum. Prodding at a lump.

In public prosecutions, Rob had seen enough of the senselessness of the world. The violence done to the innocent. It was a common complaint of the atheist. *How could a loving God …*

If miracles should happen, there had been times you might better have expected them.

Then it had been another angle. A podcast from a Franciscan priest in California. Rob fell deep into it. God as the universe. Cosmic Christ.

He read up on Ecofeminism. Carolyn Merchant. Reinventing Eden. Became a vegetarian.

And they had moved. From their house in North Perth to the coast. A tired apartment block, flanked by mansions, south of the coffee strip.

Fred thought ocean-front living was fool's gold. Endless sun in your eyes. Screaming wind. But she didn't say it. Rob wanted elevation. His hospital bed looking out over water. And in those last weeks, Rob had been content. There was pain. But she could see in his face that there wasn't fear.

Then why should she struggle to see him? To look at him?

She felt such anger in any of his talk. His daily inventory of what he had seen from his perch on the balcony. Humpbacks, their breaths like cannon smoke. A kingfisher that had visited on the railing. It was all so bloody earnest. And she tried to hide that from him. But she didn't see the comfort in it. Being stardust didn't make her feel one with anything, it just made her morose. How could anyone find any comfort in particles, in the detritus of an exploding sun. It seemed pretentious to her, or even dishonest. And she felt less and less capable of concealing it.

It was good then that he had insisted she keep working. He knew her preference for being busy, working hard. Fred would go mad sitting around the house, ruminating on existence. He didn't want to change anything for her.

Her days had been miserably tethered to the corporeal. A bulldog that had throttled someone's cat. A road accident on the outside of town.

At night she would sneak around the kitchen for water so as not to wake him, to have to talk. Rob had taken an interest in the change in her. Even in the mist of drugs he was concerned for her. Confused by it. She couldn't bear to see that either.

And she knew that was a failure, that he should have to look out for her with the weeks he had left. She had not risen to the moment. But she couldn't pull herself out of it. Couldn't even bring herself to smile. And that angered her too, what she had amounted to when it counted. It made it hard to look at her own reflection.

Every time she went through that living room now, she saw that shadow on the bed. Wished she could lie down with it, with him. That she could have that time back.

In her dreams, over and over, Fred would turn and find that Rob wasn't there. Just the dark of deeper water. With her head at the surface, she'd scan behind her. The world bright, sunlight splintered by the wet glass of her goggles. Yell his name. Head back under, a circling turn. Realise then that she was no longer over the shallows. She couldn't see the bottom. Just ribbons of light that threaded down and down and down towards the dark. Goggles fogged. She'd tear them off. Head to the surface. Turn to the beach but there was no beach. No Rob, looking down on her from a balcony. Just a dipping horizon, in every direction.

DON'T STAND SO CLOSE
TO THE WINDOW

ANGELA SAVAGE

DON'T STAND SO CLOSE TO THE WINDOW

I don't know what makes me look up. I tend to keep my eyes on the ground, a small concession to my GP's concerns about the wisdom of walking at night in an ill-lit town. On the lookout for tripping hazards – uneven pavers, protruding tree roots – I seldom glance at the houses as I pass. But that night, something distracts me. A hoot, perhaps, the flutter of wings. I raise my head. My eyes land on the silhouette of Marlene Coburn, framed by Frank Della Bosca's bedroom window. And to the right, just inside the frame, is Frank.

Of course, there's possibly a perfectly innocent reason why Marlene, married to Frank's old school friend Mick Docherty, is alone with Frank in Frank's bedroom at ten o'clock at night. But even as I struggle to think of one, Frank steps forward, puts his hands on Marlene's shoulders and kisses the back of her neck. She swivels in his arms. Frank looks poised to kiss her again when, as if sensing my gaze, he breaks away to draw the curtains. I release a breath I don't know I'm holding and, with what I excuse as an old lady's prerogative, I start to cry.

Back home I pull a notebook from the shelf, a nondescript thing stored among knitting patterns and instruction booklets. Inside is a yellowed clipping from *The Bacchus Marsh Express*. Alongside a detailed account of the Maddingley Spider's grand final victory against the Melton Bloods in 1958 is a photo of winning goalkicker Tom O'Malley and leading goalkicker Robert Blainey, arms locked around each other's necks. They wear matching grins, Robert's hair patted into submission, Tom's as ratty as couch grass.

'Good lad, Robert Blainey.' The memory of my mother's voice, reading the paper over my shoulder. 'But that Tom O'Malley ...'

'What've you got against Tom O'Malley?' I asked, though I knew the answer. Tom's mother had shot through when he was a toddler. His father had turned to the bottle, leaving Tom to be raised by his grandmother. The boy had grown up wild, though the crimes levelled against him were pretty minor. Truancy. Loitering. The odd report of blasphemy.

'An occasion of sin,' Mum sniffed, adding, 'you are not to be seen in public with that boy, Margaret.'

If only she knew.

I'd made the trip from Ballan to Bacchus Marsh to attend all the Maddingley Spiders' matches that year, supposedly cheering for my brother James, never taking my eyes off Tom. Noticing me noticing him, he took to grinning at me whenever he came off the field, one time brushing past close enough to transfer a smear of black mud from his sleeve to mine.

Still, when he turned up on our doorstep after the grand final, I assumed he'd come for James.

'Actually, it's you I wanted to see, Maggie.' He wore his trademark grin, hair askew, hands in his back pockets. 'I was wondering if you'd come to the dance with me tonight.'

I caught my breath. The grand final dance was where every girl in the district wanted to be, the hall in Rowsley booked well in advance for the Bacchus Marsh League premiers and their supporters.

'Mum says I'm not to be seen in public with you.'

'Fair dinkum?' Tom seemed more amused than offended. He glanced at the wattle that shielded our front room from the street. 'How about Bob? Will your mum let you be seen in public with him?'

'With Robert?' I rolled my eyes. 'She'd be beside herself.'

Tom chuckled. 'Bob can bring you then. He owes me one.' He started backing away. 'When the band starts playing their sixth song, meet me outside round the back of the hall, okay?'

'Start of the sixth song, right.' I marvelled at how calm my voice sounded, given the kaleidoscope of butterflies in my stomach.

I don't know how much Robert knew of the plan, but he turned up to escort me to the dance as Tom said he would, much to my mother's delight.

Before the dance itself, there were speeches and toasts to be made. I was fit to burst by the time the band finally started to play. I danced the first two with Robert, one with James, another two with Robert. Upbeat numbers that couldn't go fast enough. My cheeks hurt from the effort of smiling. When the sixth song finally started, I excused myself, bypassed the ladies' room and, resisting the urge to run, made my way outside.

In the dim light behind the hall, I saw Tom bow extravagantly and hold out his arms. The music was faint but clear. 'Love is a Many Splendored Thing'. He pulled me so close, I could not tell whose heart beat faster. It was early spring, but I had no sense of the cold. We swayed to the music of one slow song and the next. When the band picked up the pace, Tom opened the space between us, spinning me around, stomping to the rhythm.

'Who taught you to dance?' I asked between breaths.

'My nana.' He smiled. 'She said I'd never want for female company if I could dance well.'

'And was she right?'

Tom spun me close and wrapped his arms around me. 'This is the first time I've put it to the test.'

I can't recall how many more dances we had before Tom took my hand and led me into the deeper darkness beneath the redgum that overlooked the hall from a small rise. We kissed, and I felt something new happen to my body. Like being let in on a secret. It wasn't until days later, watching an electrical storm over Bald Hill, that I could find the words to describe how it felt. Like being struck by lightning on the inside.

We saw each other three or four times a week for months after that, always after dark, usually in a park beneath a tree. Once, as I left him to go home, my skin still tingling, I crossed paths with Joyce Saunders, the town gossip. I didn't think she saw Tom, as he always gave me a five-minute head start. Still, we resolved to be more careful after that, meeting further afield in the bush that fringed the town, the grunting and rustling of unseen animals adding to my excitement as we kissed in the dark.

Then Tom disappeared. We were due to meet on the bridge over the river in Caledonia Park but he didn't show up. No one seemed to know where he'd gone or why. Joyce spread rumours he'd gotten some local girl into trouble, and I couldn't defend him without my mother finding out about us. So I kept my mouth shut. My head ached with the weight of unshed tears as I waited for word from him that never arrived. I nursed my broken heart for more than a year before accepting that Tom simply mustn't have felt the same way about me that I felt about him. Perhaps the intensity of my feelings had scared him off.

I stare again at the frail newsprint photo in my notebook: the boy I loved on the left and the one I married on the right.

There was no lightning with Robert. Still, he was a good man, and we got along well for the most part. After we married, we moved into a double-fronted weatherboard cottage half-way between the main street and the Ballan railway station. Robert worked for his father, selling agricultural equipment, while I volunteered for the local St Vincent de Paul Society. Life was pleasant, if a little dull, but I counted on that changing once the children came along.

But the children didn't come. My sister married two years after us and delivered a baby within a month of her first wedding anniversary. Our fifth anniversary passed and I was still childless. I saw a specialist in Ballarat who diagnosed 'idiopathic infertility'. I had to look up idiopathic in the dictionary. It meant cause unknown.

Our parish priest suggested we adopt. But I only had to think of the girls in our district, shunted off to Melbourne, returning months later with their faces etched in grief, to know that I couldn't in conscience stake my own happiness on someone else's loss.

I continued to pray for a baby. As the years passed and my prayers went unanswered, I prayed for the grace to accept my burden. But deep down, I felt cheated. With the exception of falling for Tom, I'd always done the right thing. Surely God wouldn't punish me so harshly for so brief an aberration?

~

The apple hadn't fallen far from the tree in the Saunders family: it was Trish Saunders who told me that Tom was back in town to put his grandmother's house on the market, only hours before Robert informed me that he'd invited his old friend to dinner. I didn't expect to feel anything – it had been over a decade since that dance in the dark behind the Rowsley Hall – but as soon as I laid eyes on Tom, my body remembered his touch like it was only yesterday. Heat rose in my face and when he kissed my cheek, it gave me goosebumps.

'You look good, Maggie.'

'Still the charmer,' I said, backing towards the kitchen. 'Beer?'

'I'd prefer a red if you have it.'

I eavesdropped on Tom and Robert's conversation while I prepared the dinner, a beef bourguignon I made on special occasions. I learned that Tom lived on the south coast of New South Wales where he ran a landscaping business. That explained why, unlike Robert, Tom's body had not softened with the years. He was married, of course, and had a five-year-old, Billy. Over dinner, Robert asked to see a photo of the son. I was relieved when Tom apologised for not having one.

'Delicious dinner, Maggie,' Tom raised his glass of claret to me.

Robert also raised his glass. 'I'm a lucky man – I eat like a king.' He gave my hand a squeeze before turning back to Tom. 'So how long are you in town?'

'A week or so.'

'I'm headed to Albury tomorrow for an auction,' Robert said. 'Will I get to see you again if I'm back by Tuesday?'

'Should do, Bob.' Tom nodded. 'But while you're away, perhaps you'll let Maggie be my dinner guest at the old house.'

'Sure,' Robert said. 'But who'll do the cooking?'

Tom grinned, and I felt like a girl again. 'Maggie, how do you feel about pot luck?'

Tom's family home had been empty since his father and grand-mother moved to Melbourne years earlier. Expecting it to be grotty, I'd almost packed the rubber gloves and Ajax along with the chicken casserole I'd made for our dinner. But the place was in better shape than I expected. The floors were clean, the scant furniture free of dust and even the windows had been washed. I could tell because the coverings were missing – succumbed to old age, perhaps. Tom must've had the electricity reconnected as the lights were working. Having spent most of our time together in the dark, the irony of being so exposed was not lost on me.

'I didn't really expect you to bring dinner, Maggie,' Tom said, relieving me of my stockpot. 'But thank you.'

He put the pot on the stove but didn't light the jet.

'Would you like a glass of wine to start with?'

I found myself nodding, though I wasn't accustomed to starting with wine. Wine was something to have with the main course at a dinner party.

'To old times.' Tom touched his glass to mine.

The wine worked at the knot in my stomach. A couple more sips and I started to unwind. Tom and I talked about the old days – he asked after a few of the Maddingley Spiders team members and their girlfriends – and I asked him about where he lived. Somehow, we both managed to avoid talk of his wife and child, and of Robert.

We had a second glass of wine. Tom asked why I didn't have children. I shared with him the definition of idiopathic. I shed a tear. Tom suggested we move into the lounge room, where he made a fire in the grate. He topped up our glasses and lit some candles so we could turn off the light.

Midway through our third glass of wine, Tom asked why I'd never responded to his letters.

'What letters?'

'The letters I sent after I left town. When you didn't answer the first one, I guessed you were dark at me for leaving without saying goodbye. I wrote once a month for a year, but you never answered. I figured you'd found somebody new.'

I put my glass on the floor, not trusting myself to hold it steady.

'Did you write your name on the envelope?'

'Yeah. I thought you'd be more likely to read the letter inside if you knew it came from me. I guess I was wrong.'

I shook my head, unwilling to believe the implications. 'I never received any of your letters, Tom. Mum must've kept them from me.'

'Oh, the—' He stopped himself.

'I thought you didn't love me anymore,' I said. 'Where did you go? Why didn't you say goodbye?'

'I got a shot at an apprenticeship with a landscape gardener, a mate of my old man's. I arrived home late after I'd been with you and the guy was literally waiting for me to drive with him to Bateman's Bay. He and Dad had set the whole thing up. It was an offer too good to refuse, Maggie. I didn't have anything holding me here except you, and I thought I could convince you to follow me.'

'I would've followed you anywhere, Tom.'

We smiled sadly at each other.

'Too late now.' Tom raised his glass. 'To lost love.'

I retrieved my glass and touched it to his. 'Lost love.'

We sipped the wine. Tom leaned forward to kiss my cheek. I turned my head so that our lips met.

We should have stopped there, a single kiss for old time's sake. But I was overwhelmed by a hunger I didn't know I had. I pushed my fingers into Tom's unkempt hair and pulled him close. Suddenly, we fell into each other. This body of mine that had failed to make a baby was nonetheless good for something. My dress fell at my feet. Tom's shirt and pants followed. Still kissing, we collapsed on to the couch, releasing dust that smelled of lavender.

Later, Tom left the room to get another bottle of wine. I wrapped myself in a throw and wandered over to the window. It was a clear night and the stars over Ballan were magnificent.

'Hey, get away from the window, Maggie,' Tom said, setting a bottle on the floor by the couch. 'What if somebody sees you?'

For one reckless moment, I thought, Let the world see. Let life as I know it come crashing down around me.

But did I want that?

I joined Tom on the couch and rested my head against his bare chest, sipping the wine and watching the flames dance. I could hear music coming from another room – Tom must have put the radio on.

'"Maggie May".' He kissed the top of my head. 'This song always reminds me of you.'

I didn't know the song, but the idea of Tom thinking of me at all made my heart soar.

We sat in silence, feeling the warmth of the fire on each other's skin. I was reluctant to speak. Conversation felt too risky. But a question nagged at me.

'When you left town all those years ago, did Robert know where you were?'

The strokes on my shoulder stopped. 'You know, I didn't even think to write and tell Bob.'

I looked up at him.

He shook his head. 'What an idiot!'

Of course Robert would've told me if he'd heard from Tom. We both knew it.

Talk of Robert broke the spell between us.

'I need to go home,' I said, shimmying back into my underwear.

Tom sat forward, the blanket slipping from his muscular shoulders, candlelight turning his naked skin to gold. 'You sure, Maggie?'

'You know, my mother was right about you.' I said, removing my underwear again. 'You're an occasion of sin, Tom O'Malley.'

In the immediate aftermath of our night together, I harboured fantasies about falling pregnant to Tom, less concerned than I should've been at the prospect of cuckolding Robert. But it didn't happen. A great relief, in retrospect: I could never have handled the guilt. Tom went home to Bateman's Bay and my life returned to normal.

I finally made peace with never having children, only to fall pregnant at the age of forty-four with a change-of-life baby. Seems God does love a sinner after all. Our daughter, Jessica, recently turned twenty-eight. She lives in Melbourne these days and works for the government. She and I are close. We talk every week, though

I've never told her about Tom. She'd die if she knew – she thinks I'm so straight. No, what happened between me and Tom is a secret I'll take to the grave.

I never confronted my mother about Tom's missing letters either, though I did look for them among her papers after she died. But if she had intercepted them, she'd covered her tracks. Probably for the best, really. Losing Robert suddenly when he was sixty taught me there's no point in bearing grudges. How does the Alcoholic Anonymous saying go – that holding onto anger is like drinking poison and expecting the other person to die?

Two days after I spy Marlene Coburn in Frank Della Bosca's bedroom, I head to the station to catch the midmorning train to Ballarat, where I'm meeting a friend to visit the gallery. When I arrive, the only other person on the platform is Marlene.

She has her back to me. The sulphur-crested cockatoos in the pines across the tracks are making such a racket, she doesn't notice as I walk towards her and touch her lightly on the elbow.

She turns, frowns.

I say, 'You should stay away from the window, Marlene. What if somebody sees you?'

The approaching train sends the cockatoos into a renewed frenzy. Did she even hear what I said? She shakes her head and turns away.

I drop my hand, and whisper into all that tumult of arrival and departure, 'Isn't it beautiful to be loved?'

Author's note ~ Thanks to Alex Gionfriddo at State Library Victoria for his help with the history of the Bacchus Marsh Football League. While the Maddingley Spiders did defeat the Melton Bloods in the 1958 grand final, Tom O'Malley and Robert Blainey are works of fiction. The premiers' real leading goal kicker was W. Closter.

DESDEMONA

SARAH DRUMMOND

DESDEMONA

DESDEMONA

Otto and Desi

'It's ten past four on 6WA Radio and we've just heard from the Whaling Station. They're reporting a catch of eight whales and their ETA is approximately 1800 hours. All flensers to be at the station at 0600 hours tomorrow.'

Every day, a woman listened to this report on her transistor. She put on her raincoat and walked down to the jetty to wait for her sweetheart to return.

No man but his brother knew how Otto got such a beauty, this man with flat eyes, low-hanging ears and wonky face. He was uneasy in his bonehouse, anyone could see that. The new chum Norseman cruelly imitated his way of standing with his curled paws facing behind him, and the gunner called him a chump. And there she was, his wife Desma, or Desi for short. God help the girl. Trusting, kind but naïve. Her hair, masses of it, shiny and the colour of fine-cut tobacco, blew around her face as she waited for him on the jetty. A farm kid from the east – sheep and wheat country – whose connection with the sea was a mariner ancestor and post-harvest holidays to the coast for the salmon run.

The whale grounds were quiet during the summer months and so last February Otto and his brother Saul had driven east along the beaches to meet the swathes of salmon schools swimming towards them.

At a beach near Cape Riche they moved into a little shack behind the primary dune. They found an impromptu fish smoker made from an old fridge and Saul cleaned out the little earthen tunnel. Smoked salmon and boiled potatoes that night.

Two more days of fishing and drinking and then they were disturbed by an old International rattling along the track and into the camp. Three kids and a young woman sat astride the carvel boat on the tray. The kids, blond hair wild with dust and wind, stared at the brothers. Otto stared at the older girl with chestnut hair. She leapt off the truck and lifted her siblings down. The father climbed out of the cab, strode into the shack, looked around and not unkindly directed the brothers to remove their things.

Saul saw the quickening alert in his brother at the shack that day. He gave a short laugh. 'You're gone, aren't ya?' They dropped the sack of potatoes and cooking gear into the boot of the Premier. Otto dawdled, watched the girl cart armloads of sleeping bags into the shack.

Saul was the handsome one of the two. He married young and was now in his early thirties, his brood of kids growing in number. His wife picked him up from the pub hours after the chaser returned, saved him his driver's licence but it was always four beers in when he didn't want to leave, when Jodie arrived, welcome as a dose. She had to start her night shift soon, she'd always say. Going to sea was Saul's way of stepping off, leaving land's lap of trouble and women. Going to sea is a bit like drinking and he wanted to stay there forever.

Hiatus

In the autumn Desi and Otto went back to the beach shack. It was a honeymoon of sorts, returning to the place they first laid eyes on each other. At the tank outside, he poured cups of cool water through her hair to wash out the salt. The hazy summer skies were cleared and crispened with new rains. She told him the story of how her grandfather met her grandmother just out to sea a bit from this very beach. He was a ship's captain and man of the sea, Desi said, and her grandmother a land woman, whose family drove sheep down to the coast for shearing. They rowed the bales of wool out to her grandfather's ship the Ferret.

'So romantic,' Desi sighed, wringing the rain water from her hair, 'and now I have my own man of the sea, a whale man. An iron man in an iron boat.'

'It's a terrible thing to see them die but,' he said.

Hunting

Otto woke when the ship's vibrations changed and he knew they were at full speed and maybe already chasing. The engine beneath his bed thrummed. They'd arrived at the whale roads off the Continental Shelf. He swung off the bunk, put on his beanie and saw Saul had already left for the sonar room.

Three chasers, five miles apart, steamed east along the Shelf to meet the whales. To the west, Otto could just make out the little spotter plane gridding the sky.

Saul saw the undersea as rolling paper with the flickering needle printing black dots and shapes and mysterious languages. In his headphones he heard the whales' clacking intensify as they understood their danger. The spotter pilot bugled over the radio, all numbers and bravo whiskeys and the ship changed course accordingly. Saul sat at the sonar, tracking the travel of the whales. He watched the dots converge and knew which shape was a calf and which was a bull.

'Green 20, Range 700, Tilt 40,' he called into the transmitter, relaying the whale's position to the skipper. The ship's gears changed at Saul's command. The gunner stirred on the bridge at Saul's command.

It was Saul's reading of these hieroglyphs that dictated whatever happened next and he knew it. He also knew it was down to him if they lost a whale.

He left it to the gunner to work out the bull from the cows. The humpy bulls always hung around if a cow was killed, maybe even charged the ship. If it were a bull shot, the cows just took off. As they all do. Treacherous bitches, Saul thought.

In the chill grip of winter, when Saul saw Desi standing on the jetty waiting for her Otto, her hair wild with the dirty easterly and her face a pale smudge above the yellow raincoat, he felt envy against his brother spike his stomach.

Night Shift

Saul's wife Jodie got Desi the job at the cannery, working with whatever was in season. There Desi made friends with Narelle, a sparky, outspoken girl who wore bright makeup and who noticed everything. Words came out of her, so unthinking and refreshing after the cautious, quiet language from Desi's land to the east. Narelle was thrilling to be around and Desi contrived to be near her on the conveyor belt.

Desi twisted her chestnut hair into a tight knot and covered it in a gauze hairnet. White gumboots, white plastic apron that reached to her ankles and thick, red rubber gloves. The women watched the river of fresh green peas running past them. They watched for the rotten ones, the stones from the inland paddocks, for crickets and beetles and cigarette butts. Narelle watched the engineer fiddling with the belt shaft. Jodie watched the two young women. It was a genuine wonder that any cigarette butts made it to the concrete floor at all.

Before the hosing down and after the conveyor belt stopped, the women made pots of tea in the smoko room and hunched over ashtrays and magazines. There was no end-of-shift siren. They finished when the work was done, when the day's harvest was sorted, washed and canned. Jodie ripped down the girlie pictures from the wall and threw them with a snort into the dented chip oil drum.

'There'll be more up next week,' Narelle scoffed. 'Why bother?'

'It's the engineer,' said Jodie. 'He's reminding us who's boss.' She lit a match and threw it in the bin.

'Jesus, Jodester! Do you want to burn us all down?'

But Jodie calmly carried the bin outside to the loading bay and let the paper ladies burn.

'It's your turn. Take those boys some grub,' said Narelle to Desi. When the mulies started running, the night women often took ice-cream containers of half-cooked potato chips, hot and salt-laden, to the men who cleaned and packed the fish. It was on another floor of the factory and the set-up was different. Desi found her way there by the smell and by the stiff southerly ripping in from the Sound. Standing by the freezing brine tanks, the workers fell upon the plastic vessels of oily, salty potatoes like starving kelpies. In their tired, midnight eyes, Desi was a fever dream, an apparition.

An Open Hand but Not a Fist

'Jodie's alright. She's got to work there so we can pay off the house,' said Saul. 'But those cannery women. They're all looking for a sperm donor, you know that don't you?'

'What about Narelle?' Otto knew about Desi's new friend. 'She seems alright.'

'That slag … watch out for her. I know what she gets up to when her hubby's out on the chaser.'

'Who, Mick from the Kos?'

'He's piss-weak. Can't see what's going on under his nose. You've gotta keep 'em in line, little brother.'

'Affairs?' Desi said on the conveyor belt. 'Do the night crew really have affairs?'

'Oh, the peas are in season, oh, the beans are in season and after that, oh, the salmon are in season. Spud season. You know what Desi? I'm in fucking season right now. Of course we have affairs.' Narelle's gloved hands were quick on the black rubber as she talked. 'They're either out shooting whales or cutting them up or they're at the pub skiting about it or they're fucking sleeping. *Christ!*'

Narelle, Jodie and Desi all lurched back as a severed hand came towards them on a carpet of green beans.

Narelle stepped forward like a crow on the road. She picked up the hand as it travelled by. Jodie's hand covered her mouth. Desi heard the engine driving the conveyor belt, *whoomp whoomp whoomp*, and Jodie screaming *stop stop stop* and the engineer and supervisor laughing at their prank.

The Whaler's Arms

'Thanks for those chips, Desi.' The man looked at her with a simple hunger. No hairnet and plastic apron tonight. She wore her favourite green dress to the pub. She called it her forest dress, a sunlight filtering through emerald karris kind of dress.

She said, 'You've got something in your hair,' and reached out to find a fish scale and he laughed, reddening. Warmth came from his wanting. It was intoxicating … but that was enough. She looked around the bar to see Otto watching her with an expression mean and shamed.

'Gets bloody cold on that floor, wind comes up the channel and straight through the factory door,' he said.

She smiled and left his side to join her husband. Otto didn't talk to her and moved his body to block her from his conversation with Saul and the gunner. He seemed embarrassed by her. Stranded, Desi's eyes found Narelle, all blue eye shadow and red lippy, twirling a straw in her rum and coke with one hand and caressing a man's curly, blond head with another.

'Get over here, girl,' Narelle waved her over. 'Meet my better half, Michael.'

Otto waited until they were home before he smacked his big paw hard across her face, twice and called her a whore.

'Lie down with dogs, you get up with fleas,' he said, which she didn't really understand. Who were the dogs? Who were the fleas?

They fought. It was always about the night shift, the affairs. Him needling, trying to force a confession, she hating her own defensiveness that made her feel guilty. The arguments spiralled and flicked around viciously. They petered out somewhere close to where they began. Late one afternoon after such a session, he followed her to their bedroom and opened the door. She sat on the orange chenille bedspread. He put his hands on her knees, gently parted them. She put her hands on his shoulders as he stooped to kiss her sex, thinking him conciliatory. He straightened then so that her hands fell away and unzipped his jeans. He was fast, perfunctory. When he was finished inside her body, he zipped up his jeans, looked at her with hard, fuck-off eyes and walked out of the room.

Iron Boots

The skipper forgave Otto for missing the three am shipping-out the first time and sacked him on the second. Otto had been finding it difficult to leave for work before Desi came home from the night shift. Sometimes they were out on the chasers for fifteen hours or more, and there was no way to check on her. He lay awake in the crew quarters while Saul snored. He visioned her going into that filthy little mulie-shoveller's bedroom. The image was real. He could see the dirty yellow pillow, the full ashtray and he saw Desi stroke his hair the way she had at the pub that night.

Flensers hold a perverse dignity for their work, the work of dismantling a whale, but Otto was a chaser man and putting on the spiked boots to climb over a carcass rankled him.

'If you hadn't been so busy mooning over that silly bint, you'd still be on the chaser,' Saul said, mouthing a bourbon, and he was right, Otto thought. Now he watched a cow winched up the deck, her beautiful body buckled by gravity, her teats the size of a child's fist, disgorging milk onto the concrete. Parts of her tail were ribboned with shark bites. The guts, bone and ambergris were all pushed into the digester. No longer an iron man in an iron ship.

She climbed into bed without even washing, white with exhaustion. She slept a few hours and then woke to the drone of the spotter plane overhead and Otto shaking her. He was angry.

'You have to wake me when you get home,' he muttered. 'Otherwise ...'

She stared at him, groggy. It was the second time she felt afraid of him. But this time there was no violence in his hands and his voice was calm. It was the power of him, the potential, coiled inside him, without reason or logic.

The morning after the worst night, when Otto caught Desi speaking in a low voice on the phone, he went to work at the station and rowed out to the pontoon near the flensing deck. Divers were working on the hydraulic line the next day and the company needed someone to sort out the sharks. Otto stood on the pontoon with the company shotgun and some chunks of whale meat in a cheesecloth bag. He watched two great whites ambling around like benign goldfish. There was no sense to this. He threw in a chunk and their movements changed instantly. He thought – the way he felt whenever on a cliff top – about throwing himself in. Enough whale oil on him to bring all the fish to the party here. He threw in another chunk, close to the edge of the pontoon. He raised his shotgun, sighted the cold eye of the great white that rolled up its head to look at him.

The local sergeant, a decent man who hadn't got the memo that Otto was no longer on the chasers, stood waiting for the ships to return. Jodie had rung him first. Desi hadn't showed for the night shift and her house was all locked up. Then Desi's father, ringing from out Wellstead way, quietly laid out his concerns for his daughter. She was going to leave Otto, he said, but she wasn't on the bus. The sou'-easterly blew the whaling station's death stench over the town. It began to rain and the policeman shrugged into his raincoat, waiting on the jetty, as the chasers steamed through the heads.

AN ARCHIPELAGO
OF STARS

MARK SMITH

DEEPER WATER

AN ARCHIPELAGO OF STARS

Archie stands on the end of the jetty, pushing his bony hips against the guardrail. He spreads his arms, and the gale turns his jacket into wings. The waves lash at the pylons underneath him and spout like geysers through the gaps in the planks. He feels the jetty shudder and creak, while all around the harbour, trawler cables whistle and complain.

Steadying himself, Archie steps up onto the rail and lifts a torch out of his pocket. He holds it aloft and its beam catches the sleet in rainbow colours. He swings the light in an arc from east to south to west: a one-boy lighthouse against the storm.

'Daaaaaad,' he screams, and the wind fills his mouth and turns his voice to a howl.

The house sits snug behind the dunes, out of the wind. The yellow glow from the windows peers up at him like eyes in the gloom. Archie waits for the lightning to gash the horizon one more time before he makes his way down through the tea-trees. He slides through a gap in the paling fence and wedges the torch between the shed and the water tank. The yard is a maze of weeds and succulents. He zigzags his way to the back door, opens it and feels the rush of warmth from the kitchen.

'You're wet through,' his mother says.

'Got caught out on the reef looking for crabs.'

'Best get out of those wet things. Tea's not far off. And your uncle's coming.'

Archie looks at his mother. She's wearing her good dress, the floral one with the scoop in the back. As she turns to lift a saucepan off the stove, he sees the blusher on her cheeks and her eyes are rimmed with kohl. A musky scent fills the kitchen.

'Come on, chop-chop, mister,' she says.

Above the desk in Archie's bedroom is a painting of a tall ship, its sails straining against a gale and its port gunwale almost underwater. A wave swamps the deck and sailors with ropes tied around their waists tumble like ninepins. Archie touches his hand to the prow, a woman's torso and head. Her hair is lost in the netting and her breasts push out to meet the storm.

'Leila, Queen of the Roaring Forties,' he whispers.

Stripping to his underwear, he sits on the bed, unstraps his diving watch – a gift from his father on his twelfth birthday – and places it flat on the blankets. He inhales and exhales deeply as the secondhand jolts towards twelve, then takes one last lungful of air, holds it in his chest and lies back on the pillow. In the quiet of the breath-held world, he can almost hear his father singing in the kitchen, his tuneless voice murdering 'Under the Boardwalk'. Life is briefly full of everything that could have been: the smell of fish frying in the pan, the shuffle of dancing feet on the lino floor, his mother's laugh, his father calling him for dinner.

But the oxygen steals the memories as it thins and fades.

Archie sits up, gasps for air and looks at his watch.

Russell arrives with his usual swagger and noise. He takes up so much space in the little rooms, his shoulders too wide for the doorways, his head almost touching the low ceilings. Archie looks through the crack in his bedroom door and sees his uncle place a six-pack of beer on the table before leaning in to kiss his mother. He lifts her off her feet and her dress pulls up at the back so Archie can see her thighs.

'You smell so good, Stell,' he says

'Put me down, Russ,' she protests, but her voice says something else. She turns her head to the side and slaps him away.

'Where's my little mate?' Russell says, too loudly.

Archie shuts the door quickly and calls, 'Won't be a minute. Just getting changed.' He pushes his back against the door and takes deep breaths in and out. This is always the worst bit, this and what happens later when all the lights are out, the sounds they make together.

Dressed in a t-shirt and track pants, Archie opens the door and walks out to the kitchen.

'There you are,' Russell says, one hand pushed back through his hair and the other wrapped around his first beer. 'What've you been up to today, champ?'

'Just crabbing out on the reef. Not much about though.'

Archie sits down, placing the table between them.

'Don't be rude, Archie,' his mother says. 'Give your uncle a hug.' Archie navigates the edge of the table between him and his uncle.

'That's the boy,' Russell says, swallowing him in a hug. He smells of Brylcreem and sawdust and his jumper is rough against Archie's face. His uncle ruffles Archie's hair then holds him at arm's length. 'I swear you're getting bigger every time I see you,' he says. He lets Archie go and reaches for his beer. 'Here,' he whispers, 'have a sip.' He pushes the stubbie at Archie's mouth.

'Russ!' his mother says, glaring. 'He's too young.'

'Ah. You're never too young to start. Our old man gave Tom and me our first beer when we were just kids, younger than Archie here.'

At the mention of his father's name, the familiar Catherine wheel with all its sparks and flames begins to spin inside Archie's head.

Before Archie's mum can say anything, Russell puts his hand up to her.

'I know. I know,' he says. 'Christ knows we all miss him, Stell, no one more than me. He was my brother after all.' He looks across at Archie, who has retreated to the other side of the table. 'We'll have a little chat later, eh? The three of us together.' Archie sits silently and feels for the rough grain on the underside of his chair.

'Answer your uncle, Archie.' His mother's face has lost some of its glow. There are lines at the corners of her mouth and her smile is hidden somewhere behind.

'Sure,' Archie says. 'That'd be great.'

'Time you called me Rusty, mate. That's what everyone at the mill calls me. Rusty, like a nail.' When his uncle laughs Archie sees the dark fillings at the back of his mouth. His front teeth are chipped, and one turns at an angle.

'All right, you two,' his mother says. 'Time to set the table.'

Russell spreads his legs and pushes himself to his feet. He has to duck to miss the hanging light globe. Archie manoeuvres towards the cutlery drawer, squeezing between a hard-backed chair and the soft fabric of his mother.

'Careful, Archie,' she says.

The pot she's holding splashes drops onto her dress. She takes a sponge from the sink and lifts the dress to get a hand in behind the stain.

'Here, let me help you,' Russell says.

Stella holds the dress up and Russell, down on one knee, dabs at it with the sponge. Archie takes the cutlery from the drawer and tries not to see this small act of tenderness. He drops a spoon, and it clatters across the floor.

As they eat the meal of chops and vegetables, every sound seems accentuated to Archie: the scrape of a knife on a plate, the clack of Russell's teeth as he chews the meat, the smack of his lips as he sinks another beer. Somehow, Russell crowds out their little life with everything he does.

For Archie, these nights are like diving into a rip. He knows not to struggle but to go with it until it's done with him, find the safety of deeper water and swim to shore. His dad taught him this when he was young. Archie remembers the strength of his father's hand, the comfort of his own hand inside its grip, as they stood knee deep in the breaking waves.

'See,' his father had said. 'There where the sand is churned up? The water's got to channel out somewhere. Back out to sea.'

Together they had pushed through the breakers until the sand disappeared under their feet. Archie felt the fear inside him, but the presence of his dad gave him confidence to breathe easy, to slide and stroke, slide and stroke. When he looked back over his shoulder, the beach had all but disappeared, but his father was right there.

'See how easy it's taken us,' he'd said. 'That's what it does if you're not careful. It creeps up on you and changes everything. It'll take you further and further out but if you wait and see it through, don't panic, you'll be okay.'

Out beyond the breakers, they'd floated for a while and gathered their breath. This is the part Archie remembers best. They filled their lungs and dived into the dark blue sea. Deeper. Deeper. Deeper.

'How's school, young fella?'

'Archie!' His mother nudges his arm. 'Your uncle asked you a question.'

'Sorry?'

'Jesus, Archie. You've gotta wake up, son,' Russell says shooting a worried glance at Stella. 'School. I asked you how school was going?'

'Good. Yeah, good,' he says, catching his breath.

'Never took to it myself,' Russell says, relaxing his gaze. 'Left when I was fifteen.' Just like last time, and the time before that, he tells them how hard he works at the mill, how he should be off the floor by now, using his smarts to guide the business, if only they saw his potential. Archie knows every facial expression that goes with this story – the firm jaw, the shake of the head, the raised eyebrows and the look of bewilderment.

After the dishes are done and stacked away, Archie says goodnight and heads for his room. But he knows he won't make it. There have been too many glances exchanged between Russell and his mother, too many nods and unspoken words. His uncle had gone to the couch too readily, moved to one side to make space.

'Archie?' his mother says. 'Let's have a little talk, just the three of us.'

He hesitates.

'Come on, mate, your mum and I have got something to tell you.' Russell's voice has lost some of its cheeriness. He pats the cushion on the couch.

They sit facing the television, Archie in the middle. His mother slips her arm around his shoulder, and he turns to her. Up close he can see the little streaks of grey in her hair and her breath smells of wine. But it's Russell who speaks first.

'Listen Archie, you know it's been more than a year since your dad went missing.'

Three hundred and eighty-four days, Archie thinks.

'Like I said at dinner, son, it's time we moved on. He'll be at peace now.'

'But they never found any sign of him. Nothing,' Archie says, his eyes fixed on the model ship on top of the television. His father somehow made it inside a bottle, and it remains a wonder to him.

'No, they didn't, you're right. But we have to accept that he's not coming back. It's been too long, mate.'

The model has three masts and faded yellow sails.

His mother places her soft hands on either side of his face and turns him towards her. Her eyes well with tears.

'It's time to let go, darling. For both of us.' She looks past him to Russell and nods.

'Listen, Archie,' he says. 'I'm always going to be here for you and your mum. She needs support and you know I've been helping out a lot recently.'

In his head, Archie fills his lungs and dives, stroking slowly and deliberately into the dark green below. The pressure builds in his ears as he drops deeper but he pinches his nose and puffs his cheeks to equalise.

'So, your mum and I have been talking and we think it would be a good idea if I moved in for a while. Just to see how it goes, ya know.' Russell's voice is muffled by the weight of the water. 'Apart from anything else, I can help out financially. The insurance money is running out and there's your education to think of. Maybe a boarding school in a couple of years' time.'

Deeper and deeper he strokes until all the light has left the room and there's just the faint murmur that might be someone talking or might be the movement of another body in the darkness below.

'Just until we get things settled,' his mother says, 'Russell will sleep in the spare room. It'll be good to have someone else around, won't it, Archie?'

Archie is deeper than he has ever gone before.

His mother's head is tilted at an angle. Lines furrow her forehead. 'Archie?'

'Your mother's talking to you, son. You need to answer her.'

Archie reluctantly glides back up towards the light, breaks the surface and fills his lungs.

'Sorry, Mum. What did you say?'

'This is important stuff we're talking about here, mate,' Russell says. 'Your mum and I are worried about you. You keep drifting off. That's why she wants me round more. Reckons you need a man about, now that your dad's gone.'

'Can I go to bed now, Mum?'

His mother purses her lips then ruffles his hair. 'You're tired, little man, aren't you? We'll talk in the morning.' She leans in and kisses him on the cheek.

As Archie stands up Russell's big paws wrap themselves around his thin arms.

'We're going to be a family, Archie, just like it was when your dad was here.' His uncle pulls him in and Archie feels the rough stubble scratch against his face. 'Go on then, off you go,' he says. 'I'll see you in the morning.'

When Archie stands, it's like walking on the heaving deck of the *Leila*. He puts his foot down but the floor isn't where it should be. He staggers a little but then rights himself, finds the door to his room and pushes through, closing it tightly behind.

'He'll be okay. It'll just take some time,' he hears his uncle say.

'I'm not so sure, Russ. His teachers say he's distracted at school the whole time. Sits at his desk looking out the window.'

'He needs some sort of distraction, something new. Maybe I could take him down the mill on weekends, show him the ropes.'

Archie lies in bed with the lamp directed up to the ceiling where he has pinned a map of the coast and the ocean dropping a hundred miles to the south. He scans all the shoals and islands, the archipelagos shaped like necklaces, the fathoms marked in tiny numbers on lines as thin as a spider's web. He imagines the way the currents weave their way through these obstacles, how they might eddy around protected shores, how they could carry a swimmer with them. A swimmer who could hold his breath a long time. In a dozen places he has stuck little stars that will glow in the dark when he turns off the lamp.

The house falls quiet, but Archie can hear the murmurings of

Russell, his voice too big to whisper. Above it all though, he hears the deep, continuous roll of the ocean, its fury muffled by the sand dunes.

He switches off the lamp and the stars shine above his head, each one a possibility, each one a little lantern to hope. They will glow until he sleeps, until the world stops swaying and moving under him, until the *Leila* finds a safe harbour, until his father comes home, and he doesn't have to hold his breath anymore.

SONGS AND ALBUMS BY PAUL KELLY REFERENCED

SONGS AND ALBUMS BY PAUL KELLY REFERENCED

'Before Too Long', *Gossip,* Paul Kelly and the Coloured Girls, Mushroom, 1986.

'Deeper Water', *Deeper Water*, Paul Kelly, White Lable Records, 1995.

'Don't Stand So Close to the Window', *Under the Sun*, Paul Kelly and the Coloured Girls, Mushroom Records, 1987.

'Down to my Soul', *Foggy Highway*, Paul Kelly & the Stormwater Boys, Gawd Aggie / EMI Music, 2005.

'Dumb Things', *Under the Sun*, Paul Kelly and the Coloured Girls, Mushroom Records, 1987.

Foggy Highway, Paul Kelly & the Stormwater Boys, Gawd Aggie / EMI Music, 2005.

'Every Fucking City', *Roll on Summer* EP, Paul Kelly, EMI Music, 2000.

'Feelings of Grief', *Stolen Apples*, Paul Kelly, EMI Music, 2007.

'From Little Things Big Things Grow', Paul Kelly and Kev Carmody, *Comedy,* Paul Kelly & the Messengers, Mushroom Records, 1991.

'From St Kilda to Kings Cross', *Post*, Paul Kelly, White, 1985.

'Gathering Storm', *Smoke,* Paul Kelly with Uncle Bill, Gawd Aggie / EMI Music, 1999.

'God Told Me To', *Stolen Apples*, Paul Kelly, EMI Music, 2007.

'How to Make Gravy', *How to Make Gravy* EP, Paul Kelly, White Lable Records, 1996.

'I'll Be Your Lover', *Words and Music*, Paul Kelly, Mushroom Records, 1998.

'It Started with a Kiss', *Words and Music*, Paul Kelly, Mushroom Records, 1998 (after Hot Chocolate, 'It Started with a Kiss', Errol Brown, *Mystery*, Rak Records, 1982).

'Just About to Break', ... *Nothing but a Dream*, Paul Kelly, EMI Music, 2001.

'Leaps and Bounds', *Gossip*, Paul Kelly and the Coloured Girls, Mushroom / White Lable Records, 1986.

'Look So Fine, Feel So Low', *Gossip*, Paul Kelly and Maurice Frawley, Paul Kelly and the Coloured Girls, Mushroom / White Lable Records, 1986.

'Love is the Law', ... *Nothing but a Dream*, Paul Kelly, EMI Music, 2001.

'Meet Me in the Middle of the Air', Paul Kelly & the Stormwater Boys, Gawd Aggie / EMI Music, 2005.

Music for the feature film *Lantana*, Paul Kelly, Stephen Hadley, Bruce Haymes, Peter Luscombe and Shane O'Mara Paul Kelly Band, 2001.

... *Nothing but a Dream*, Paul Kelly, EMI Music, 2001.

One Night the Moon: Original Soundtrack, Paul Kelly, Kev Carmody and Maireed Hannan, 2001.

'Right Outta My Head', *Stolen Apples*, Paul Kelly, EMI Music, 2007.

'Sleep, Australia, Sleep', single, Paul Kelly, 2020.

Smoke, Paul Kelly with Uncle Bill, Gawd Aggie / EMI Music, 1999.

'Special Treatment', *Building Bridges. Australia has a Black History*, compilation album, CAAMA Music, 1989.

'Special Treatment', *Hidden Things*, Paul Kelly & the Messengers, Mushroom / White Lable Records, 1992.

Stardust Five, Stardust Five, EMI Music, 2006.

Stolen Apples, Paul Kelly, EMI Music, 2007.

'Stolen Apples Taste the Sweetest', *Stolen Apples*, Paul Kelly, EMI Music, 2007.

'The Lion and the Lamb', *Stolen Apples*, Paul Kelly, EMI Music, 2007.

'To Her Door', *Under the Sun*, Paul Kelly and the Coloured Girls, Mushroom Records, 1987.

Ways & Means, Paul Kelly, EMI Music, 2004.

'When I First Met Your Ma', *Hidden Things*, Paul Kelly & the Messengers, Mushroom / White Lable Records, 1992.

'With Animals', *Nature*, Paul Kelly and Walt Whitman, EMI Music, 2018.

OTHER WORKS REFERENCED

Michael Dwyer, 'Divine Ideas', *The Age*, 6 July 2007, theage.com.au/entertainment/music/divine-ideas-20070706.

Paul Kelly, *Don't Start Me Talking: Lyrics 1984–2012*, Allen & Unwin, 2012.

A.B. 'Banjo' Paterson, 'Clancy of the Overflow', *The Bulletin*, 1889.

Walt Whitman, 'Song of Myself', 1892.

Walt Whitman, 'Starting from Paumanok', Part 12, *Leaves of Grass*, 1855.

'The Parting Glass', Scottish traditional song, 1770s.

CREDIT NOTICES

CONTRIBUTOR BIOGRAPHIES

CONTRIBUTOR BIOGRAPHIES

Robbie Arnott is the author of *Flames* and *The Rain Heron*. His third novel, *Limberlost*, will be published in October 2022. He lives in Hobart, Tasmania.

Alice Bishop is a writer from Christmas Hills, Victoria. She was named 2020 *Sydney Morning Herald / The Age*'s Best Young Australian Novelist for *A Constant Hum*, written about her hometown's experience of bushfire aftermath.

Zoë Bradley is a writer based in Naarm/Melbourne. Her work has been featured by *Kill Your Darlings*, *Overland*, Writers Victoria and ABC Radio National. Her short stories have placed in multiple awards, including the Grace Marion Wilson Emerging Writers Competition, the Rachel Funari Prize for Fiction and the *Overland* Story Wine Prize.

Sam Carmody is a novelist and WAM Award winning songwriter from Western Australia. His first novel, *The Windy Season*, won the 2017 Readings Prize for New Australian Fiction, and in 2018 he released his debut EP, *Shadow in the Dream*. His work appears in the anthology *Lines to the Horizon: Australian Surf Writing* (Fremantle Press, 2021) and he is currently based in Albany, Western Australia.

Jake Cashion was born in nipaluna/Hobart on the island state of lutruwita/Tasmania, where he currently works and resides.

Lorin Clarke is the creator of the award-winning observational audio fiction series, *The Fitzroy Diaries*, three series of which have been to air on ABC Radio National, as well as being released as a podcast. Lorin writes regularly for children's television, and her children's book *Our (Last) Trip to the Market* was published by Allen & Unwin in 2017. She also writes the fortnightly Public Service Announcement column for *The Big Issue*.

Claire G. Coleman is a Noongar woman whose family have belonged to the south coast of Western Australia since before history started being recorded. Growing up near Boorloo, and now living in the hills near Naarm, she writes fiction, nonfiction, drama and verse. She has published three novels and a non-fiction book. Claire has also written for many publications including *Meanjin*, *The Saturday Paper*, *The Guardian*, *Australian Poetry*, *Griffith Review*, *Chicago Review* and *Spectrum*.

Sarah Drummond grew up in a whaling town on Menang Country on the south coast of Western Australia. Her books *The Sound* and *Salt Story: Of Sea Dogs and Fisherwomen* are published by Fremantle Press.

Laura Elvery is the author of two short story collections, *Trick of the Light* (2018) and *Ordinary Matter* (2020), which won the 2021 Steele Rudd Award for a Short Story Collection at the Queensland Literary Awards. She has written for *Griffith Review*, *The Saturday Paper*, *Overland* and *Meanjin*. Laura has a PhD in creative writing and literary studies. She lives in Brisbane.

Kirsten Krauth is a writer, editor and arts journalist based in Castlemaine, Victoria. Her second novel *Almost a Mirror* (Transit Lounge) was shortlisted for the 2021 SPN Book of the Year Award and the Penguin Literary Prize, and named in the Best 20 Australian Books of 2020 by *The Guardian*. Her first novel was *just_a_girl* (UWA Publishing). She is currently working on the Almost a Mirror podcast, a mashup of pop and post-punk music, fiction and documentary. She has written for *The Saturday Paper, Sydney Morning Herald* and *Overland* magazine. She was the editor of *Australian Author* and *The Victorian Writer* magazines, and has been managing editor at Writing NSW for over a decade. She was highly commended for the 2021 Blake Poetry Prize with her poem 'Pencils From Heaven'.

Julia Lawrinson has written more than a dozen books for children and teenagers, many of them award-winning. She is now completing an occasionally comedic memoir entitled *How to Avoid a Happy Life*, under the mentorship of US writer Howard Norman.

Matt Neal is an award-winning ABC reporter, as well as being an author, musician (The 80 Aces, Doctor & The Apologies), songwriter, podcaster, film reviewer, blogger (Movies8MyLife), screenwriter and playwright. He grew up on dairy farms in south-west Victoria and still lives in the region with his family in Warrnambool. He co-wrote his first book, *Bay of Martyrs*, in 2017, and his podcast Can You Believe It? has been explaining the unexplained since 2019.

Bram Presser is an award-winning author from Melbourne. His stories have appeared in *Best Australian Stories, Award Winning Australian Writing, The Sleepers Almanac* and *Higher Arc*. His 2017 debut novel, *The Book of Dirt*, won the 2018 Goldberg Prize for Debut Fiction in the US National Jewish Book Awards, the 2018 Voss Literary Prize and three awards in the 2018 NSW Premier's Literary Awards: the Christina Stead Prize for Fiction, the UTS Glenda Adams Award for New Writing and The People's Choice Award.

Mirandi Riwoe is the author of the novella *The Fish Girl*, which won Seizure's Viva la Novella V and was shortlisted for the Stella Prize and the Queensland Literary Awards Fiction Prize, and the novel *Stone Sky Gold Mountain*, which won the ARA Historical Novel Prize and the QLA Fiction Prize. Her work has appeared in *Best Australian Stories, Meanjin, Review of Australian Fiction, Griffith Review* and *Best Summer Stories*.

Tim Rogers is best known as the songwriter and front man of the hugely popular rock band You Am I, which produced platinum-selling albums with record sales of almost one million worldwide, and was the recipient of ten ARIA awards. He also regularly performs and records solo, and with several other bands. Tim is now the lead singer of Australian punk rock icons Hard-Ons.

Angela Savage is an award-winning writer, and CEO of Public Libraries Victoria. Her debut novel, *Behind the Night Bazaar*, won the Victorian Premier's Literary Award for Unpublished Manuscript, and all three of her Jayne Keeney PI novels were shortlisted for Ned Kelly Awards. Angela's short stories have been published in Australia and the UK and she won the 2011 Scarlet Stiletto Award for short crime fiction. Angela holds a PhD in Creative Writing. Her most recent novel, *Mother of Pearl*, is published by Transit Lounge.

Jock Serong is the author of six novels, most recently *The Settlement*, and the founding editor of *Great Ocean Quarterly*. He writes for *The Monthly, The Guardian, Surfing World* and other publications. He lives with his family on Victoria's west coast. He has decided against a career in prawn processing.

Mark Smith is the author of four novels: *The Road To Winter, Wilder Country, Land Of Fences* and *If Not Us*. *Wilder Country* won the 2018 Australian Indie Book Award for YA. He is also an award-winning writer of short fiction, with credits including the 2015 Josephine Ulrick Literature Prize and the 2013 Alan Marshall Short Story Award. His work has appeared in *Best Australian Stories, Review of Australian Fiction, The Big Issue, Island, The Victorian Writer* and *The Australian*.

Neil A. White was born in Melbourne and educated in Australia and the United States. He is the author of the novels *Closure, Turn A Blind Eye* and *Something for Bebe*, and a number of award-winning short stories. He and his wife live in Dallas, Texas.

Gina Williams (AM) is a Balladong (Noongar) woman with links through her grandmother's line to the Gitja people of the East Kimberley. She writes songs almost exclusively in Noongar language. With less than 400 speakers of this language left in Western Australia, Gina brings (with guitarist and collaborator Guy Ghouse) a modern take on ancient traditions, matching powerful storytelling, guitar brilliance and that incredible, incandescent voice. Gina is a five-times winner of the WA Music Industry Indigenous Act of the Year (with Guy Ghouse); winner, Aboriginal Category, 2017 West Australian of the Year Awards; and Inductee, 2018 West Australian Women's Hall of Fame. She is the author of *Kalyakoorl, Ngalak Warangka* (*Forever, We Sing*), published by Magabala Books.

Michelle Wright lives in Eltham, Victoria. Her short stories have won and been shortlisted in numerous awards including *The Age* Short Story Award, and have been published in Australia and internationally. Her short story collection, *Fine*, was shortlisted for the Victorian Premier's Award for an Unpublished Manuscript and published in 2016 by Allen and Unwin. She was recently awarded an Australia Council residency and spent six months in Paris researching her first novel, *Small Acts of Defiance*, which was published by Allen and Unwin in June 2021 and HarperCollins US in July 2022.